# The Mermaid's Quest

J. D. MANDERS

authorHOUSE®

*AuthorHouse™*
*1663 Liberty Drive*
*Bloomington, IN 47403*
*www.authorhouse.com*
*Phone: 1 (800) 839-8640*



*Cover Illustration by Susan Shorter.*
*Interior Illustrations by Lily Manders*



*Published by AuthorHouse 11/13/2015*

*ISBN: 978-1-5049-5619-2 (sc)*
*ISBN: 978-1-5049-5620-8 (hc)*
*ISBN: 978-1-5049-5618-5 (e)*

*Library of Congress Control Number: 2015916867*

*Print information available on the last page.*



*This book is printed on acid-free paper.*

# Table of Contents

# Preface

In another book, *The Fairy Child,* I explained how when I had mobilized with the U.S. Army National Guard in 2004, I wrote a story to entertain and comfort my daughters, Sarah and Lily. I sent it home a chapter at a time, and my wife read it to them. The book was about two little girls, very similar to my own, who went on an adventure in a magical fairy land while their father was deployed. They had to be brave and learn to do what was right in order to save a kidnapped fairy prince. Along the way, they picked up friends – an elf warrior named Elwin and of course the fairies themselves. The story became very popular with my children and their friends, so I should not have been surprised when they asked for me to write another story for them not more than three months after I had returned from Iraq.

The idea for this story originated with a trip we made to the beach shortly after I had come home. I remember distinctly the discussions we held about fairy folk that lived near the water, and I told them a story of how Sarah and Lily were taken by mermaids and returned just in time for a tropical storm, just like the storm we ourselves later avoided when we left the beach a few days early. I told them other tales as well. We often read fairy tales such as *The Chronicles of Narnia*, *the Hobbit*, and *Peter Pan*, and when no books were handy, such as while on vacation or while camping, we would invent make-believe tales to amuse ourselves. At one point after getting back from vacation, I sat down and wrote out an outline and even started on the story my children requested. But having been away from home for more than a year, I had a lot to catch up on, and my job was increasingly demanding. Soon, the business of life crowded out my writing, and though I occasionally thought about the story, it remained unfinished for the next five or six years.

Then in 2011, I was called up again to serve with the U.S. Army National Guard, this time in Afghanistan. Between 2005 and 2010, I had received my commission as an officer and became a company commander. This made my life rather hectic, and I had little time to think about doing anything else than preparing for our mission. But my children were insistent. They had come to expect me to tell them stories no matter where I was. Some months later, once things started to settle down at my base, I spent a few minutes each evening working on this new story. Luckily, it was already fairly advanced. As company commander, I had much less personal time than I had during my previous deployment. I traveled more and was very busy, but you will never imagine how much time you have if you spend time writing instead of watching movies or playing cards. Even then, it took me the entire deployment to complete the story I had already started. Soon after returning from my second deployment, I published my first book. Naturally, Sarah and Lily wanted to see the new book in print as well, which I am happy to present.

I wrote these stories at first merely for the amusement of my own children, but I quickly learned how many other military families benefited from them. Fairy tales have the ability to provide healing in ways that other kinds of stories simply don't. By taking you into another world, fairy tales help you escape from suffering and disappointment. By helping you believe in fairies and other supernatural creatures, fairy tales build up faith that there are forces out there trying to help you. And by ending happily, fairy tales provide hope that everything will turn out all right in the end. Military families, as with many others, experience separation and disappointment on a regular basis. Like the Soldiers who serve, their children and spouses sacrifice greatly for our nation. My hope is that these stories help to comfort children bearing separation while teaching them to be strong and good. If the stories can help even a handful of such families, the cost and labor associated with their publication will have been worth it.

I thank again the many people who have helped make this second story a reality. I thank Sarah and Lily for their inspiration and encouragement and for supporting the troops by going with me to talk about their experiences with other military families. I thank Lily especially for providing artwork to include in the book. I deeply appreciate my wife, Christy, who continually pushed and encouraged me in seeking publication. I also wish to thank Katie Warren for editing support and numerous helpful comments. Most of all, I thank God for the opportunity to help other Soldiers in some small way.

J.D. Manders
June 2015

# 1

# *The Sandcastle*

Sarah's and Lily's father had been home from the war for only a few weeks when the entire family decided to go to the beach for vacation. He had left the previous year to serve with the U.S. Army in Iraq. While he was gone, the girls stayed home with their mother, who often did not have much time to entertain them while she served as father, mother, and maid, all at the same time. As a result, she often left them to their own devices. While playing alone in their yard during just such a time, the girls had some fantastical adventures and claimed they had visited fairyland, met elves, and fought witches and goblins. The story of these adventures appears in another book, *The Fairy Child.*

Their mother never really believed those adventures had happened. Sarah and Lily tried many times to show her the traces of the fairy market or the old stump where they said the palace was, and they often went driving around looking for the witch's cottage. But their mother could always explain away any fairy signs as natural occurrences. The fairy circles were mushrooms. The fairy dust across the doorstep was a snail trail. The fairies flying were lightning bugs. Besides, Mother would argue, the girls were not absent long enough to have adventures, a fact which they could not explain, for in their mind they were gone for days. After many months of politely arguing the point, Sarah and Lily quit trying to explain, accepting that their mother would never believe.

Now that Daddy was home, everything had returned to normal, and Sarah and Lily no longer brought up their fairy adventures. Their encounters with the fairy folk had more or less ceased, although they sometimes thought they had seen the fairies wandering about keeping an eye on the children and protecting them from the revenge of the goblins. Sarah had sometimes thought that the goblins might return, but neither she nor Lily had ever seen a sign of them. They had seen several signs of the fairies. They occasionally saw insects flying in formation when the fairies were riding them to keep watch on the house. They sometimes found fairy guard posts in the trees or the garden, where fairies hid when watching the girls play. They also found fairy dust across the doorstep where the fairies had protected them. Such signs let Sarah and Lily know when fairies had visited and reminded them that guardians continued to look after their old friends. Otherwise, the girls had gotten on with their lives and returned to school without much disturbance or any further adventures.

In some ways, after their father returned, there was no need for such adventures. Now that their family had reunited, the girls' real life was exciting enough for them most of the time. With Daddy back from the war, Sarah and Lily were spending more time with him and less time playing alone in the yard or going on fairy adventures. He would take them to the park, push them on the swing, or go bike-riding with them, and although fairies may have watched them, they never came near. The fairy folk almost always prefer to reveal themselves to one or two children at a time rather than a large group of people, especially big people who tend to talk loudly and make a lot of noise. So they never showed up when Sarah and Lily were with Daddy.

After their father had been home for a few months, they decided to go to their favorite resort on the South Atlantic Coast. Daddy wanted to get away one last time before returning to work, and he chose a spot where he had vacationed as a child and where the family had often gone before his tour in Iraq. It was an exciting trip for the girls, especially since they were back with their father again. It was a long drive to the coast, but they talked and read and listened to music in the car to pass the time, and the girls continued to quietly play their fairy games all the way. Finally, the rows of palm trees, sand-filled yards, smell of salt, and sounds of the surf let them know that they had arrived at the beach.

Sarah and Lily loved the beach, but for very different reasons. Lily, who was now nearly seven, loved to swim. She loved to catch the waves on her boogie board, walk through the breaking waves to the calm waters, and play in the shallows. When she got bored of swimming in the ocean, she would swim in the hotel pool, where she could see clearly underwater and would not tire from fighting waves. She and Sarah were both very good swimmers. Always curious, Lily loved to seek out the crabs and periwinkles digging holes in the sand and try to catch sting rays or jellyfish in her pail while wading. She was the more social one and would often play with neighboring children on the beach, running up and down from one family to another. She would play and play in the sun until her short-cropped blond hair turned a shocking white and her skin was bronze from head to toe.

Ten and a half with long brown hair, Sarah sometimes swam and occasionally went exploring with Lily, but what she really liked to do was sit on the beach under the umbrella and read, especially when next to her father. They would sit and read, then go out and swim to cool off, then return and read some more. This always bothered their mother, who liked to take long walks on the beach or go shopping at all the tourist places that sold shells or shirts or mugs. When Sarah did swim, she liked to get on a float in the calm, deep water past the breakers. She would just lie there rolling up and down until the waves caught her and brought her onto the strand, often hundreds of yards from where she started. Then she would go out and do it again.

What both Sarah and Lily liked most of all about the beach was building sandcastles. Daddy had taught them how to build sandcastles when they were very young. They always wondered whether he should have been an architect or engineer. Perhaps it was the history buff in their father that drew him to sandcastles, for he was always reading about ancient castles and medieval warfare. He taught them about how to mix sand and water to get the right consistency, how to use the pail to build towers, how to dig tunnels without making the castle overhead crack, and how to build the foundation so that really tall towers did not collapse. He also taught them how to angle the towers along the wall so that they could protect or fire at every angle, how to build the moat so that it protected the keep, and how to build gate houses so that the entry way into the castle had the strongest protections.

It was no surprise, then, that on the first day after they arrived at the beach, one of the first things Sarah and Lily did was build an enormous sandcastle, with Daddy helping. They spent many hours working on it. First, they built the keep itself, with a high tower that was almost as tall as Lily. Then, they built the crenelated inner walls high around the keep, with large towers on the corners and a gate house. Then they built a small village on the outside of the keep, with another wall surrounding it with smaller round towers every so often. Then the castle spread out into the countryside, with a further wall surrounding the common fields, each wall shorter and thinner than the one after it. Driftwood, shells, and twigs formed the doors and drawbridges and flags. As usual, there was a moat, dug from a large tidal pool up through the outer walls to surround the keep with a deep river. Over the moat they built a bridge that crossed to the gate house. Every time the tide came in, it would wash up into the moat and around the castle. There was even a little boat house far away from the castle by the sea, with a little protected road leading to it.

Of course, all the time Sarah and Lily built the sandcastle, they took breaks to swim and read and eat. Mother brought down a picnic basket from the hotel room filled with sandwiches, sodas, and fruit. Then, she would make them take a time out to rest at least half an hour before going back in the water, and she would ensure that they were coated with sunblock, to keep them from getting sunburned. They obeyed, even Daddy, but then they went right back to work on the sandcastle.

At last, the castle was finished. It was a grand achievement and caught the eyes of all the passing people, who praised it for its realism. In fact, Lily thought that it was a little too real, especially after it sat for a time – they left it standing after they had finished and then went on to swimming and other fun. Amazingly, no one tore it down as so often happened. Usually, some teenage boys would kick it over, or the policeman would run it over with his four-wheeler. The girls thought the fact this did not happen to their sandcastle was a tribute to its greatness. They would go out to look at it from time to time, and Lily could have sworn that she saw lights in some of the houses and in the keep itself, and that it looked at times like there had been traffic in and out of some doors. She showed Sarah, who agreed that it had a lived-in look, although they never saw people or fairy folk, but whenever they showed Mommy or Daddy, their parents never saw anything, or they would explain it away as an active imagination.

"Look at the tracks going up to the castle," Lily said.

"Dear, those are crab trails," Mommy would say.

Or, "Look at the lights twinkling in the tower," she would point out to Daddy as the sun set, turning the sea into a shimmering reflection.

"That's neat how the sun reflects off that shell," Daddy would say.

"Why won't they believe when I show them?" Lily asked her sister later.

"Grown-ups never see anything magical," Sarah said.

"Never?" Lily asked.

"Well, rarely," she responded. "At least, that's what happens in books. Like in *Peter Pan*, when Wendy's mother does not believe in Peter until the end, or in *The Lion, the Witch, and the Wardrobe* when only the Professor believes Lucy's story."

Sarah read a lot and knew all of the fairy stories. After she explained their parents' reaction using books, Lily understood.

"Do you think fairies have moved into the castle?" Lily asked.

"Probably not," Sarah said, "since we built it only yesterday. Maybe some passed this way and stopped to stay in the castle."

"It is very grand. It is the kind of place fairies would choose to live. I mean, there are so many rooms and towers where they can stay. Everything is already the right size for them. Sarah, what kinds of fairies live near the beach?" Lily asked.

"Well, there are fairies that live near water, such as brownies or pixies, who might live near a well or an old house. You might hear about some pools or wells that are enchanted themselves, that grant three wishes or try to drown you. Like the famous Fountain of Youth that Ponce De Leon found in Florida. Some say Indian spirits inhabited it and made it magical. You don't really hear about these being near the sea, though. There are also spirits that live in water such as water horses or kelpies, which are sort of sea demons, but they usually live in shallow water. Some live on land but play in water, such as selkies, which are people who change their form into otters. Mostly, though, you hear about creatures that actually live in the sea, such as mermaids or a hippocampus."

"Hippo?" Lily said. She had liked hippopotamuses ever since she had seen one at the zoo when she was little.

"Not hippopotamus; hippocampus," Sarah explained. "It's like a seahorse, only with a regular horse body instead of a fish tail. And you have other sea creatures, giant crabs and squids and such. But most of these never go on the beach. It would have to be a traveling fairy, just like the others we saw."

Sarah and Lily continued to watch the castle, coming often late at night to see if it was still there and still being visited by fairies. The sandcastle continued to stand and continued to have what Lily called "little visitors," although she never actually saw anyone. The weather stayed calm for a long time, the sea receded, and the tide stayed low, so the waves did not even get high enough to wash out the castle, which stood on a dune with a tidal pool in front of it. There were times they would find a piece of wood floating in the water that looked just like a barge, or Lily would notice some part of the castle that had been improved or moved, but it was nothing she could say with absolute certainty.

Still, the girls' vacation drew on, and their interests soon returned to swimming and exploring and relaxing on the beach. The next day, they went out to swim. At first, they could not hear over the crashing waves, but finally they got far out past the breakers. As usual, Sarah got on her raft to float. After swimming about and looking underwater with her goggles, Lily hung onto the side as they talked quietly about the fairies and about Daddy getting home. Suddenly, Sarah stopped talking.

"Do you ever get the feeling that someone is watching us?"

"You mean like from the beach?" Lily asked, turning her head. There were several families on the beach, including their father and mother sitting under an umbrella. Daddy waved at them, while their mother yelled something about not getting out too far.

"No, it feels like it is coming from behind us, out to sea," Sarah replied. There were a few boys swimming somewhat next to them down the beach, but the boys had not been behind them.

"Well, there was that boat that went by a while back," Lily said.

"No, it's been more recent," Sarah said.

"Maybe there is a boat far out where we cannot see it," Lily wondered. "You remember that story Dad used to tell about drifting out so far on his raft he saw an ocean liner. There could be a large ship that is watching us, but we can't see it because of the waves."

"Maybe," Sarah said. "But it feels more like it is coming from under the waves."

Lily slipped on her goggles again and stuck her head in the water, looking around. The water was a dark green, but she could still see the bottom a few feet below them. She saw the sand, some kind of seaweed, and then she saw the fin of a fish of some kind. It looked rather large and startled her. She pulled her head back out.

"Sarah, there's a fish down there," Lily said.

"Of course there's a fish," Sarah replied. "It's the ocean."

"No, I mean a really big fish," Lily explained.

"Is it a shark?" Sarah asked, sitting up and pulling her legs onto her float.

"I don't think so. I did not see the head, but it did not look like the fin of a shark. You know how shark fins are sort of moon shaped and move from side to side. This one was flat and moved up and down. More like a dolphin. It was also the wrong color. This one was green, not gray or blue," Lily explained

"Well, let's not take any chances," Sarah said and started to paddle back to shore.

"At least we know what made you feel like you were being watched. It was obviously some animal looking at you from the sea," Lily said.

"I wonder," Sarah said. It did not seem at all like a fish was what had given her the feeling of being watched. It felt more like a person watching. But there were obviously not any people nearby. Lily was probably right, and it was all in their heads or it was some sea animal looking at her.

"Sarah," their father called as he waved at them to return to the beach.

Sarah and Lily swam back to shore, climbing out on the beach as the sun was setting. They waded through the tidal pool and crawled up the side of the dune where their sandcastle still stood. As it got darker, the castle took on an ominous look. Perhaps it was the gathering clouds of the storm forecasted to hit the coast. It seemed to get much darker much quicker than expected. There were black clouds across the sky, leaving the remainder of the horizon a strange gray hue. Or perhaps it was the wind having blown some of the fresh sand off the castle so it looked a little worn, a little rough in places. It did not look like the new castle they had built. Or maybe it was how the incoming tide had eroded away some of the outer walls and towers, making them look like they had melted. Many of the quaint little farm houses they had sculpted around the castle were nearly gone now. But mostly it was how the light seemed to gleam and flicker through the windows in the high tower, making it look as though it were inhabited, as though someone were watching television or lightning were striking in that high tower. It sparked their imaginations.

"We need to get back to the room. It is going to start raining soon, and we need to get off the beach," Daddy said.

Daddy was waiting on them with a towel, and Sarah and Lily started to dry off. He had already folded up the chairs. Mother had gone ahead to the hotel room, and they soon followed, dragging a cart full of towels, clothes, floats, and chairs with them as they went.

Sarah, Lily, and Daddy got in the elevator, which started to go up to their room high up in the hotel. Through the window on the elevator, they could see the beach, and between two buildings across the street the very slice of beach on which they had sat and played for several days.

Sarah could just make out their sandcastle. It was like a large yard had been fenced in, and they could easily make out the keep and moat and towers. Still no one touched it. No one ran over it. The police driving their four-wheelers down the beach went around it. The mean kids who went around destroying everyone else's sandcastles simply went around theirs. The waves did not reach it, and the tide always seemed to stop short. It was as though the whole outpost was protected from harm, or that it was invisible to those who were not there when they had built it.

Sarah wondered about the sandcastle long and seriously. It was strange, almost inexplicable, how quickly the castle seemed occupied by fairies. But she was not sure what to make of it. No one had contacted them, as had happened in the past. As her parents got ready to go out, she sat on the balcony watching the castle. There was something spiritual there, almost fairly like, but she could not put her finger on it. The surf pounded hypnotically. After a while, she became distracted, and went inside to get dressed for dinner.

# 2

# The Old Fisherman

It had been a family tradition that whenever they went to the beach, they went out to eat at a fine seafood restaurant at least once. Daddy said that it was all part of the seagoing experience and hoped that it would broaden their tastes. They would always find some out-of-the-way or even not-so-out-of-the-way restaurant that served not only red snapper or tuna or flounder, which Sarah and Lily would usually try, but also shrimp, scallops, lobster, crab, oysters, and clams, which they did not like as much.

On this occasion, Daddy found a restaurant a little ways down the beach on a point that stuck out into the water. The family drove past all the hotels and beach houses until they came to shady lanes of trees strung with Spanish moss. Then they passed horse pastures. Finally, they reached the other side of the island, where there were more expensive houses facing a public pier, along which stood numerous stores and restaurants. It was like a public square, only instead of a courthouse there was a bay with sailboats, motorboats, yachts, fishing trolls, and tour boats moving in and out or tied at one of the docks or boathouses.

The family arrived early so they could go to one of the area's attractions – an old lighthouse – before the sun finally set. It was one of the oldest lighthouses remaining on the southeast coast. They climbed the hundreds of steps to the top and then went out on the upper deck. They could see for many miles, the storm having cleared off to the north somewhere. They could see the end of the point, the bay, and the beach stretching for many miles. They could also see more and larger ships coming and going. The girls had not been aware when they were swimming that this part of the shore was such a busy place for non-tourists. There were many homes that they could see through the trees – everything from large plantation houses to beach houses up on poles – and they realized that the area was actually a home to many people who lived and had jobs there.

Once the sun dipped down and dusk approached, someone in the interior of the lighthouse turned on the light, which started to circle behind them, sending its beacon into the night. It was glaringly bright, but only lit up the sky, not the ground below them. Since they could not see as far with it getting dark, they climbed down the stairs and stopped at the lighthouse keeper's home, which had been converted to a museum. There were glass cases full of old telescopes, wood from sunken ships, some items from recovered treasure, pistols and muskets, tobacco tins, and pipes. In a corner stood a dummy dressed in traditional lighthouse-keeper garb. On the walls were pictures of the lighthouse, ships, and a lot of people involved in local history.

An old man was standing in front of one group of pictures. He was dressed in a large yellow rain coat and black galoshes. He had a short, rounded beard and a bald head. Out of his mouth hung a long pipe – unlit. He was carrying on a conversation with one of the curators of the museum.

"I'm telling you, that picture's mislabeled. The name of the ship was the *Handley*. I should know. I sailed on her for many seasons as a lad fishing all throughout these waters.

"And this man, whom you've identified as the captain, was only so for the last few seasons it worked these waters. The captain before that was James Hugh. He later went to South America and supposedly became a pirate. That's him in the background of that picture. He was one of the ones that insisted on this lighthouse after his first ship sank right off these waters, and you don't even mention him. He said something had distracted him in the waters and that a lighthouse would help fix the problem."

"Thank you for your comments, sir," said the curator. "We will make sure to correct the plaques. If you have pictures you would like to donate, we would make sure they are included in the collection."

"No, no pictures. I kept very few traveling from port to port, and most of the ones I had were destroyed when the *McDermitt* sank back in '71."

The old man turned to leave, and Sarah, Lily, and their parents looked at all the pictures and items. Then the girls asked their parents for money to put into the penny press – a machine that pressed a picture and slogan into a penny. They collected pennies from all of the spots they visited. This one had a lighthouse on it with the name of the town.

After a few minutes, Sarah's and Lily's family finally left to go to the restaurant, which had a dining room right on the waterfront. They sat eating and talking for a while. Naturally, Sarah and Lily finished before their parents since their portions were smaller and they only picked at some of the more exotic food their father had ordered. After a few minutes of sitting and talking, they asked if they could be excused to walk on the pier or visit some of the shops.

"OK, but stay in sight of the restaurant where we can see you," their mother said.

Sarah and Lily walked along the pier, looking in store windows. After a while, they got bored with window-shopping, and walked the other way past the restaurant to where a ship was docked. Beyond that, the dock ended. There, at the end of the pier, was the old fisherman from the lighthouse sitting on the edge of the dock and smoking his pipe with his head surrounded by smoke. He held a fishing pole extended out over the water.

"Hello," Sarah, who was the bolder of the two girls, said to the man. Lily sat down a little ways down from the man and tried to look under the pier.

"Good day," said the fisherman, who continued to draw on his pipe and look out over the water without turning his head.

"We overheard you in the museum saying that you were a fisherman on several ships out of this port, like the *Handley* and *McDermitt*," Sarah said.

"Yes, that's right," he said after a pause. Still he stared ahead.

"And James Hugh was the captain of both?"

Another pause. "Yep."

"And he became a pirate?" Lily asked. She started thinking of *Treasure Island* and buccaneers and buried treasure.

"So they say, but I never confirmed it," he said through his pipe.

"I did not think pirates still existed," Sarah said.

"They do, but not like in books. Anyone who robs ships is a pirate. Most of them today live in Asia or Africa, not in the Caribbean, and they use modern ships and weapons."

"So why did he become one? Couldn't he make it commercially?" Sarah asked.

"Actually, he was one of the finest sailors I ever knew," the old man said.

"Yet his ship went down," Sarah said.

"That was not his fault," the man said quickly.

"What was it that distracted him?" Sarah asked.

"He said it was something supernatural, but no one ever believed him," the fisherman said.

"Something supernatural? Really? Like what?" Lily asked.

"He said it was mermaids," the man said.

"Mermaids? Really? Are there mermaids around here?" Lily returned. She jumped up and looked out into the water, as though she would see one right then waving to her.

Finally, the man turned his head toward her and took his pipe out of his mouth.

"Supposedly, there are mermaids all along this coast. Been incidents similar to Captain Hugh's on and off for centuries, with ships crashing on rocks and sailors being rescued by pretty young girls. That's why he wanted the lighthouse, to scare them away or give sailors direction so that they would know where to swim when their ships went down," the man said.

"Wow!" Lily exclaimed.

"It's also why he ended up leaving for South America and becoming a pirate. Some say he was searching across the whole ocean for the mermaid he saw that night. That always sounded like a lot of romantic nonsense to me. I always thought it was because people made fun of him all the time and he wanted to go somewhere to build up a reputation as a tough guy," the old fisherman said.

"But I always read that most mermaid sightings were actually manatees," Sarah said.

"There may be some," he replied, "But how many people do you know that would mistake a fat manatee for a beautiful girl?"

"It always did seem unlikely," Sarah mused to herself.

"I can't say exactly if that is what he saw, but I do know that there are some in this area. I have seen them. Once, when I was a boy, I remember looking off to the starboard of the vessel I was sailing on and seeing two female bodies smiling up at me from the sea about a dozen yards away. That was only a few miles from here. My shipmates tried to convince me that it was all in my head since a boy of twelve imagines things, but I know what I saw. I was wide awake, and the sea was as calm as it is now. There is no chance I would make that kind of mistake," the fisherman said.

"Why would mermaids be around here?" Sarah asked.

"Don't you know where you are?" the man asked.

"No, sir," Sarah and Lily both answered together.

"You're right on the edge of the Bermuda triangle," he replied.

Sarah and Lily stared at him blankly.

"Davy Jones! What do they teach children in school? The Bermuda triangle is a region from the coast of Bermuda to Florida where a lot of unexplained things happen, like ships and planes disappearing for years only to reappear unharmed later, or compasses going wild and people getting lost. Whether the mermaids actually cause disappearances by abducting people or whether they simply take advantage of people being lost and crashing, there is no doubt that sightings of mermaids in the triangle are much higher than elsewhere," the man explained.

"What causes the triangle?" Sarah asked.

"No one knows exactly what causes it. You hear different theories. Some say it's some kind of psychic phenomena that makes people forget things. Others say it's just atmospheric conditions because of the location of the islands or some kind of mineral deposits in the earth that make electronics quit working. Personally, I think it's because the lost island of Atlantis is somewhere beneath the waves," the old man said.

"I have heard of Atlantis," Sarah said. "I saw a history show on it one time."

"The philosopher Plato mentioned it once; said it was a land far advanced for its time that was destroyed by a natural disaster and sunk beneath the waves. It was a mystical place, built of concentric rings like some kind of machine. If it was automated, there might be some works that draw other machines or interfere with them somehow. Or it just might be some kind of magic, if you believe in that sort of thing," the old man said.

"Please, sir, tell us about the mermaids," Lily said.

"Well, they are quite beautiful, of course, with the body of a girl or woman above the waist and a fish below. There are mermen, too, but no one ever sees them. It's the womenfolk that are curious and come to the surface all the time to find handsome young men. They say that the mermaids are not too bright, and not too interested in anything not related to them. They often do not understand how water affects mortals. Yet most are friendly enough and are glad to help young men when they are in trouble, although a few have been known to drag men down to the bottom just for spite. Personally, I think this is because they were jilted. Still, a lot of this is rumor. I have only seen two, and then only from a distance. But the legends are there in Hans Christian Anderson for anyone who wants to read about them," the old man said.

"Sarah! Lily!" they heard their mother call.

"Guess we better go," Sarah said, "But nice talking to you."

The old fisherman waved at them as they walked off, and then returned to his fishing. Sarah and Lily looked back fondly at the dear old man.

"Who was that?" Mother asked.

"Just an old fisherman. You may remember that he was in the museum," Sarah said.

"Ah, yes," Daddy said.

"Well, that was nice of you talking to him," Mother said.

The girls and their parents returned to their hotel. All the time, Sarah thought about what the old man said, about the mermaids and the Bermuda triangle and Atlantis. She wondered if they had seen a mermaid and not known it. It might explain her feeling watched. But it did not explain the weird occurrences near their sandcastle. No mermaid could fit in that. That had to be something else, but she knew not what. Still, Sarah turned those thoughts over in her mind as she sat on the balcony listening to the waves and looking at the distant sandcastle, which was still standing despite the incoming tide.

That night, another spiral of the storm came in, with pounding rain and high winds. The weatherman said that it was a tropical storm. Everyone was evacuating the area. After several hours of watching the weather, Daddy deemed it safe enough to stay the night but said they would leave the next day. It looked like their vacation was coming to an end, but as it turned out, their adventure was just beginning.

# 3

# Past the Waves

The following day, the storm had abated, but the waves were very high, reaching eight or ten feet, which was very high in that part of the Atlantic. They would have been a boogie boarder's delight. During the lull in the rain, while Sarah's and Lily's parents cleaned the room and loaded their baggage in the car, they said the girls could take one last walk on the shore or go swimming. The waves were still very elevated, too high for very good swimming; otherwise, they would have immediately gone out in the water. Lily wanted to go to the pool to swim, but Sarah insisted on wading and enjoying a final breath of salt air. They walked along the beach a ways. The wind was blowing hard, kicking sand up in their faces, and the sound of the waves crashing drowned out their conversation. Yet the water was warm on their feet and legs, and the sand between their toes was soft and light.

The girls walked several hundred yards out along the beach and then returned to where they had played and swam the first day of their vacation. Strangely, their sandcastle still stood there where they had built it. Although the moat had widened a good deal, knocking down a few of the outer walls and towers, and the waves had destroyed some of the outbuildings, the keep itself with its tall tower and walls stood strong. It seemed like the wind and rain had not touched them at all. They looked more or less as the girls had left them the previous night.

"That's odd," Sarah said. "The storm did not even touch the main castle. It's almost as if there is magic or something protecting it. Not even the rain touched it. There's almost a circle around the entire area."

"Perhaps the fairies are there after all," Lily replied.

"Maybe. Still, it seems so strange...," Sarah said.

"Sarah, look! There is a little girl out drowning," Lily shouted over the roar of the waves.

Sure enough, they could see bright blond hair and a flesh-colored back floating in the waves, face downward. Then the face came out of the water, all sputtering. 'Help!' a distant voice shouted.

"Quick, we should help her," Lily said, and immediately ran out into the water.

"Wait. Be careful," Sarah started to say, "The waves are too high." But since Lily had already plunged into the water, she decided someone had better go with her to protect her and keep her safe, so she quickly followed her despite her own sense of danger.

Sarah and Lily swam out after the little girl, but it always seemed that she got farther and farther out, as though the tide were taking her. Sarah had always heard about undertow and only imagined that this was what it was like – being carried swiftly out to sea by a little current. As they got out past waist-high waves, it became a struggle to keep up. The waves were getting higher, and they had to force their way through them. At first, they could turn sideways or dive into the waves and get past them, but it got harder and harder, and each wave seemed to knock them back a few feet even as the current drew them forward. Still, they could see the little girl just beyond the next wave. When they got past that wave, she was beyond the next one. If only they could have pushed a little harder, they could have reached her.

"Sarah, the waves are getting too big," Lily said. Then she saw an enormous wave coming right down on them. "Uh-oh!"

The wave crashed down on their heads, finally knocking the girls off their feet and tossing them under the water. But they were already near the end of the breaking waves, and though they were knocked down, they did not go far back, for the current now seemed to be pulling them out to sea. Sarah's head broke the water coughing. Lily came up next, but she had gotten enough of a warning to hold her breath. They could barely touch the bottom now. They looked around and saw the little girl once again just beyond their reach. Sarah thought she could grab her, so she started doing strokes out on the open water, up one wave and down another. Lily followed. But now, it was clear that the little girl was not just floating away from them, but swimming away from them.

"Wait, crazy," Sarah shouted. "The waves are too strong; you will drown."

It was then that Sarah noticed that the beach was getting smaller. It was not just that it was getting farther away, although they were drifting out to sea and were now very far from land. The beach was actually getting smaller and the waves were getting bigger. The perspective was simply wrong for the size they were and the distance they should have been. It reminded her of their visit to fairyland once so long ago. It was almost as if they were unconnected from the beach and that the sea was fairyland.

"Here we go again," Sarah told herself.

Sarah looked back at the ocean, which was getting larger. It was almost as though they were now far out at sea, and they could no longer touch the bottom. The sea pitched and rolled in large peaks and vallcys, sometimes several dozen yards high. After a few minutes, they could no longer see the beach. All around them was the sea, and the girls quickly lost all sense of direction.

Suddenly, Sarah and Lily saw the little girl stick her head above the waves, looking far too perky and sassy for having just been washed out to sea.

"Follow me," the girl said laughing, and then dove under the water. As she did, a large fish or fish tail flipped up into the air before plunging into the water.

"Did you see that?" Lily asked.

"Yes, but I would have never have believed it," Sarah said.

"It was a mermaid," Lily replied. "Should we follow her?"

"I don't know," Sarah said. "In stories, mermaids lure fishermen and sailors to their deaths. They are really not so nice. Or rather, it is like the old fisherman said. They are not very bright and not very thoughtful of others. We certainly would not want to drown just because she does not know that people need air to live."

"It seems like she wanted us to follow. I mean, if she were luring us, would she have shown herself as she did just now or keep acting like a drowning girl?" Lily asked.

"I suppose keep acting," Sarah said.

The girl's head came up out of the water and smiled at them, and she waved her arm for them to follow. Sarah started to say something to find out what she wanted.

In the end, the waves gave Sarah and Lily no choice in the matter of whether or not to follow. An enormous swell rose over their heads and plunged down, pushing them under the water. Down, down, down, they seemed to go, thirty or forty feet at least. It was too far for them to get back up to the surface to catch a breath. They were both pretty good at holding their breaths after many years of practicing at the neighborhood pool, so they were able to hold out for several minutes as they tried to swim back up. Finally, Lily released her breath, letting the bubbles of air slip to the surface. After another few seconds, she would breathe in the watery death and drown.

Just then, the mermaid – for mermaid it was, tail and all – swam between them and the surface, casting a cloud of bubbles over them like fairy dust. Then she swam up to Lily and kissed her on the cheek, as one friend kissing another. Suddenly, Lily breathed in, but it was air she breathed, not water. Or maybe it was water, but it tasted and seemed like air. It was as natural for her as though she were in her own atmosphere. The mermaid did the same to Sarah just in time to prevent her from drowning. The girls both could breathe normally, and breathe they did, even as they stopped swimming up.

"Follow me," the mermaid said again, and then swam off in a gradual downward direction. Once again, it was strange that they could hear her. Sarah knew that according to the principles of sound and her experience swimming, they should not have understood her. Sound did not carry underwater, at least not very well. It would have sounded distant and muffled. Yet here her voice sounded just like it did on the surface. It must be some kind of magic, she thought.

"I guess we should follow," Sarah said aloud, her own voice sounding as clear as day. Lily nodded.

Sarah and Lily swam after the mermaid. Despite the fact that they were both pretty good swimmers, it was slow going. They had no tail and could not keep up with the mermaid, but she was patient, always coming back to get them or to guide them past some difficulty or choice in direction.

"This way," the mermaid would say, as they swam around rocks or avoided an octopus or swordfish.

Sarah and Lily followed the mermaid across shallow bars and wide ruts filled with seaweed, past beds of shells and over coral, around a manta ray and through a school of minnows. As they were still in the shallows, the sunlight was still bright overhead, and the waves moved over their heads. They could feel the waves pull and push them. It made swimming very difficult, for they always felt the tide pulling against them.

The little mermaid was swimming forward at a rapid speed, stopping only occasionally to show the way or to let the girls catch up. It was very difficult and tiring for Sarah and Lily to keep up, and they were soon winded, and their legs ached from kicking.

Finally, Sarah stopped and said, "Wait a minute."

The mermaid swam back. "Yes?"

"You must give us more time to rest. We are not used to swimming so far and so fast," Sarah insisted.

"Oh, I forgot you are not of the merpeople. This place is very open. It is not safe. Just ahead is a little sheltered cove. Let us continue to there, and then you can rest," the mermaid said.

So the mermaid, Sarah, and Lily swam forward until the ground rolled beneath them again, and they turned south along the ridge. On the far side of the ridge a little ways down was a small cut, like a little bay, with rocks and coral growing all around it so that one could swim up from every direction and not see it – except for overhead, which was open to the sky.

"We can stop here," the mermaid said.

Sarah and Lily sat down on a rock and started rubbing their calves, as the mermaid seemed to float effortlessly above them. She appeared to be looking around as if nervous or anxious, swimming from one side of the cove to the other.

"Well, if you are taking us somewhere, we might as well get to know each other. My name is Sarah, and this is Lily."

"Yes, I know," the mermaid said. "Or rather, I was told so. Still, it is nice to be formally introduced."

"How did you know? Who told you?" Sarah asked.

"Triton, the king of our people. He told me where to find you and sent me to bring you to him," the mermaid replied.

"Where did he learn our names or know where we were? What does he want with us?" Sarah asked.

"I'm not sure I can answer that. He just knows things like that. As to why he sent for you, he did not tell me. He often keeps his own counsel," the mermaid said.

"And you are ..."

"Oh, my name is Scallop. Scallop Nauticus," the mermaid said.

"So where are you taking us?" Lily asked.

"To the great mer city of Coral. It is just over a few more ridges, right before the drop off."

"Why did you act like you were drowning to get us to follow?" Lily asked.

"I do not understand. I was merely swimming and showing myself to you. It is true that I wanted you to follow, but how was I to get you to do so if you did not see me?" she asked.

"But you yelled for help," Lily said.

"Yes, I yelled, 'Help us.' I meant my people, of course," Scallop said.

"It's like I said," Sarah said quietly to her sister. "They don't understand people, so they do not know that a girl swimming in the ocean yelling help would appear to be someone drowning. At least, she didn't."

The girls sat resting a moment more, while Scallop continued to swim from one side of the cove to the other, looking about in different directions.

"Why are you looking around so much?" Sarah asked. "Are you lost?"

"Lost? Why I have been swimming in these waters since I was a fry," Scallop said.

"Well, then, is there someone following us?" Lily asked.

"That is what I am trying to see. I mean, there is no one following us that I know of, I am just being careful. Over the past couple of months, the Sand Witch has been invading our lands and trying to take over our domain. It is said that she has spies all over. Even some of the fish have gone over to her side, if you can believe that a fish would turn on the merpeople. Anyway, Triton said for me to make sure we weren't followed," Scallop said.

"Wow, a Sand Witch," Sarah said.

"It makes me hungry," Lily said with a slight giggle.

"Come, we had better get moving again. We still have a ways to go," Scallop finally said.

Sarah and Lily took off swimming again, once again going over ridges and coral formations. At one point, Scallop waved them behind some rocks as they watched a shark swim by. They watched quietly as the beautiful but deadly creature coasted effortlessly over some seaweed and then disappeared the way they had come.

"Sharks are not always friendly and attack merpeople from time to time," Scallop told them later, "although we sometimes use domesticated sharks to pull things. You just have to be careful because they are dangerous in the wild."

The troop continued to swim until they came to a great trench; at least it seemed so to the girls. The land sloped downwards, and far away they could see it sloping back up to another plateau. They trailed behind Scallop as she followed the lay of the land downwards.

"Why don't we just swim across?" Lily asked, who was getting tired again.

"It is easier for large fish and enemies to see us if we do that. This way we blend in with the ocean floor," Scallop answered.

Sarah and Lily followed Scallop down. As the sun became more distant, it grew a little dim, and the water got cooler. They could still see the bottom, but now everything had a blue tint to it. They came to a flat valley floor, which was covered in sea weed. They swam across it, stopping every now and then when Sarah or Lily noticed some fish or crab moving about the weeds. Finally, they started their ascent on the other side, climbing up the slope through vigorous kicking and swimming.

After about fifteen or twenty minutes of the hard climb, Sarah, Lily, and Scallop reached the top. Not far from the top of the slope was a large coral formation about twenty or thirty feet high that ran in either direction as far as they could see. At the top were jagged formations like the spikes or wire that sometimes ran on top of a stone wall. The top came much closer to the surface of the water, not more than ten or fifteen feet from what they could see.

Scallop turned right at the bottom of the coral wall, and swam along it for several hundred yards. By this point, Sarah and Lily were exhausted, nearly worn out and ready to quit, so the two were swimming much slower.

At last, Scallop, Sarah, and Lily came to a large opening in the coral shaped like an arch. All manner of fish and sea creatures along with mermen and mermaids were streaming in and out of the arch. Above it was situated a large structure built of rock and coral, like a gate house. They could see faces through large slits in the structure, like people peering through a window. At the base of the gate house, for that is what it was, were several mermen wearing helmets shaped like conch shells. Each held a trident and a net, the chosen weapons of the merpeople, and each had another object made of shell hanging by a rope around their necks. As they approached, they could see that it was shaped like a horn.

"Welcome to the city of Coral," Scallop said.

# 4

# The Mer City

Scallop swam up to the gate, followed by Sarah and Lily. When the guards saw Scallop, she motioned to Sarah and Lily and spoke something silently to them. Two of the mermen with tridents put the shell horns to their lips and blew four short blasts, a signal perhaps to King Triton that his invited guests had arrived.

One of the guards called out to the crowd at the gate, "Everybody move!" and gestured with his hands to separate, and people quickly made a lane for them to enter. They passed a line of merpeople of all shapes and sizes, as well as various carts being drawn by fish or other creatures. Scallop, Sarah, and Lily passed up through the middle and past the gate until they stood within the city walls.

It was like some magical dream Lily had when watching her fish tank at home. She used to pretend that her fish were in the ocean and that the castle at the bottom was an underwater kingdom. She used to imagine that they all lived in a city under a log or in the plants, where they raised their children and swam and played. When they swam in schools, she used to believe they were really in school, swimming around learning lessons about the ocean. When they swam up to the surface, she pretended they were coming up to talk to her, and she sometimes even talked back. Sometimes when she swam she used to pretend she was a fish doing the same things. Now, here all her dreams came true, except that instead of fish they were mermaids and mermen.

The mer city stretched before them. There were tall spires of coral in the distance like skyscrapers. Closer, there were rough apartments built into coral or stone walls, with small huts of wound driftwood twigs and houses made of large shells or sand bricks around the edge. It was relatively flat here, and they were fairly close to the surface - certainly no more than a hundred yards - and they could clearly see the sun above them, seemingly just above the surface of the water. This made the entire city a very bright place, even when clouds passed over the sun, for the water was as clear as in a pool, and the crystalline nature of the surface magnified and intensified the sunlight as it sparkled throughout the deep. Although there was a slight blue tint, as there was everywhere they went in the undersea world, here it was near to the bright yellow or orange of the outside world. It really made them feel close to home and a little lighter at heart than the dark depths they would later see.

Although they were on the bottom of the sea, and sand was everywhere, it was by no means a desert. In some places, seaweed or underwater lichen grew instead of grass, with larger plants, anemones, coral, or sea urchins serving as trees and bushes. There were plants, fungi, algae, and other sea creatures with flowers and thorns, leaves and branches. There were as many colors or even more than you would see in a flower bed at home. Some plants were obviously growing wild on the sides of the thoroughfare; others were part of sculpted gardens or were in rows like cultivated vegetables, in front of or behind the various houses.

Smooth stones and ground shells formed the street, which went nearly straight through the middle of the town with avenues running off to the side every so often. Along the streets flowed every manner of conveyance they had ever considered at the bottom of the sea. Mermen and mermaids swam along the streets as though walking, but there were often two or three levels of traffic, with some swimming pretty near the bottom, some swimming ten or fifteen feet over their heads in a different direction, and some swimming ten or fifteen feet above that. There were some who swam far above, but no one, Sarah noticed, swam directly out of the city without going through the gate. She would later learn that some magic protected the city and prevented anyone from entering or leaving from above.

In addition to those merpeople on 'foot,' there were some riding on sea horses, some on horses with fins instead of hoofs – the hippocampi – and some on eels, rays, or large fish. There were some driving carts pulled by seahorses or manta rays. Most seemed to be very busy, taking goods to market or traveling to and from jobs. About half seemed to be soldiers, riding on hippocampi or walking, all armed with tridents. There were also undersea chariots of great wealth, made of shell, coral, and gold, which carried the wealthier merpeople to their homes.

The merpeople themselves were as different as one person to another. There were some with blond hair, some with brown, some with black, and some with red. Some had dark-colored skin, some light. Although they did not have clothes to separate them – for no one needed clothes in that warm water, and they would hardly last unless made of some water-resistant material – some did wear different hats or jewelry or bikini tops and vests made of shells or other materials. They also had different-colored tails. Some were plain green, blue, or gray; some were white with red splashes or red with white splashes. Some had stripes of fluorescent blue or red. It was really amazing the amount of variety in their colors. Sarah and Lily had never before considered that it would be so, since movies always depicted mermaids as being more or less the same.

The three of them proceeded on through a large market square near what must have been the middle of the city.

This appeared to be where most of the people were going. Throughout the square were numerous tents or booths selling various items. Next to one booth were pallets full of building materials such as shale, shell, or coral made into blocks or bags. A large merman was picking up a cartload of shale blocks. At one tent, a mermaid sold jewelry made of shells and precious metals. Another mermaid stood haggling over a beautiful comb made of shell. At another booth, there was a stand with piles of various foodstuffs such as seaweed, creel, kelp, and sea cucumbers. Next to it was a stand like a butcher shop, where a man with a knife cut up fresh fish, crabs, lobsters, clams, and other delicacies. The trio continued to swim through the market without stopping, other than pausing to look for a few seconds.

Finally, Scallop and the girls made it to what Sarah could only describe as the wealthy part of town. Here, the houses were much larger and more often made of coral and less of sand or debris from the sea. Each was clearly marked with a number, unlike the shabbier houses on the edge of town. There were wider spaces between the towering houses, which left more room for vegetation. There were large sea plants leaning over the streets like elms over wide avenues. The vehicles they saw on the streets were nicer, and more likely to be held together with metals such as gold or silver.

Scallop swam up a walkway to one of the taller houses. An older mermaid with gray hair pulled back in a bun met them on the walk.

"Here is the key to the house," she said as she handed Scallop a set of keys made of a shiny, dark stone, marble or obsidian from the look.

"When will King Triton wish to see them?" Scallop asked.

"He is busy, but given their importance, probably not more than a day or two. I have let him know they are here." The old mermaid turned to Sarah and Lily. "In the meantime, you are to stay here. You are, of course, free to wander throughout the city. Do not go outside the gates, however, and do not go too close to the drop off. I will send someone to fetch you when you are wanted. This could come at any time, so it's probably best not to be gone for too long at one time. You will find food and lodging within.

"Scallop, you are to wait on our visitors, keep them company, and keep them out of trouble. You will accompany them for their interview," the old mermaid concluded.

"His wish is my duty," the young mermaid replied.

The old woman with a bun then left them to investigate the house. Sarah and Lily decided after such a long swim that they should rest and eat before they did anything else, so they all went into the house. As promised, there was a cabinet with fresh food. Scallop fixed them a seaweed salad, which the girls both found very good, although a little less crisp than what they were used to. Scallop offered them some fish, but since she ate it raw because there were no fires to cook with, they passed at first, politely saying "no thank you" as their mother had taught them.

"You must eat some kind of meat. You will need energy," Scallop insisted. Finally, Sarah and Lily agreed to try a fish tenderized and seasoned with some kind of undersea herb. They found it a little slimy, but the flavor finally overcame their repugnance. Lily ate the entire meal. Sarah only ate enough to be polite as she had always had problems eating slimy textures. The one thing they missed was bread, yet Scallop served some kind of fungus or plant that closely imitated its texture and, spread with a little jelly from jellyfish, was actually quite tasty.

After they ate their fill, Sarah and Lily went out on the balcony, which sat high above the city, yet faced away from the market and toward the drop off. Below, they could see rather large houses and numerous avenues fading away until they seemed to stop on the edge of a cliff. The city seemed to sit quite literally on a shallow bar near the edge of the continental shelf. Just past the last house, the land just dropped off into a deep abyss, too dark to penetrate. Lily could only imagine the strange creatures that inhabited that cool nothingness at the bottom of the ocean. But the lightness of the shallow sea before them quickly distracted her. In front of them, directly out from the drop off, they could see the ocean extending out as infinite as the sky, but much bluer, almost a deep azure that faded into purple. In the distance, they could sometimes see a number of creatures: a whale, squid, or other creatures circling like eagles or hawks; a school of fish taking wing as a unit like a flock of birds; or jellyfish rising like balloons into the sky.

"Oh, I wish I could go there," Lily said.

"It is forbidden for us to go without permission," said Scallop. "It is very dangerous there. The most dangerous sea creatures, many of whom most of us have never seen or named, live beyond the drop off."

Sarah and Lily then looked to the south, and there they saw what must have been the palace of King Triton. It looked a little like a sandcastle, but the walls were embedded with shells buffed to a shine like jewels. Above it, they could see a tower of coral that reached almost to the surface, which commanded a view of the entire city. They looked for some time at that tower, believing that was where they would soon go.

Then Sarah and Lily turned their heads northward, where more of the city stood. They could see the tall spires of coral, which, evidently, marked the business section. Looking into the windows of the buildings nearest them, they could see mermen and mermaids moving back and forth. In the closest building, which was more thick than tall, they could see a mermaid handling some object. After a while, they could tell it was a large, flat shell, on which she wrote with a narrow knife of obsidian similar to a pencil.

"That is the record center," Scallop said. "There are hundreds of tablets such as those going back hundreds of years. This is how we remember the past and preserve knowledge."

"We have something similar," explained Sarah as she described paper books made from tree pulp and colored ink made from dyes.

Finally, after a long rest, Sarah and Lily wished to go exploring around the city. At first, Lily pushed them to go in the direction of the drop off, but quickly found every road going that way blocked by houses or by gates. The few houses near the edge were very large – it was evidently a great privilege to own a home overlooking the drop off, just as lakefront property is of higher value in our world – but even these were well protected by high walls. There appeared to be only a handful of public gates out to the drop off, and these were usually locked. They took the rules keeping them from the edge seriously, yet even as they approached, Lily could see the darker ocean depths beyond, tempting her.

Sarah, Lily, and Scallop continued northward through the high coral buildings, stopping at a stand to get a treat of some kind of flavored cream. They came to a large park in a clearing surrounded by buildings, with a large fountain in the middle bubbling air instead of water. On one side of the park were a merry-go-round and some kind of springy material being used as a trampoline. There, merchildren were playing happily, shouting in delight as they rode on the artificial, brightly colored sea creatures of the carousel or bounced across the trampoline. Across from the park was a large building used to house the school. As Sarah and Lily came to learn, just as a church is really the people and not the building, the word "school" itself here meant the children, who were more often than not swimming around in a group on a field trip to learn about plants or animals of the oceans. Sarah, who was the more linguistic of the two girls, noted the relationship between a school of learning and a school of fish.

The merchildren in the park stopped to look at the girls, and one mermaid, presumably the teacher, pointed to them and spoke authoritatively. She was evidently telling them about the strange people visiting them from the surface, which everyone seemed to know were visiting. It was this way throughout the entire city. Although all the merpeople were polite, Sarah and Lily received many stares of wonder at the strange, finless creatures that swam in their midst. Most of the children returned to their play. A few came up to the girls and started drilling them with questions.

"Where did you come from?"

"From the other side of the surface," Sarah answered. Some of them seemed to know only in theory that there was a world without water, and she had a hard time convincing some of the younger ones that it was not a myth.

"How do you swim without fins?"

"You cup your hands together so that they are like fins, and you kick your feet," Lily said. She demonstrated for them.

"Why do you not have fins?"

"In our world, when you walk where there is no water, fins would not be very useful, so God gave us legs and hands, so we can move easier on land," Lily replied.

"What is it like above the surface?"

Sarah described the sun, the land, the air, and their own civilization. There were enough similarities that most seemed to grasp it immediately. The hardest thing for her to explain was fire, since the merpeople had none. The closest thing they knew was lava coming out on the ocean floor, and she was able to use this to make them understand that fire was like that but could be controlled and moved around in containers, and that they used it to cook and keep warm.

Eventually, the children grew tired of the questions, and one by one returned to playing. Sarah and Lily left the park and continued north until they came to the large coral wall that surrounded the city. They followed the wall around for a long time. Every so often, there was a tower on the wall, accessible by a door from the city. The towers reached high up toward the surface of the water above them. They could see more of the guards with their tridents and tall shell helmets far above on the tops of the towers and along the walls. They passed three of these towers as they continued their circuit, and still the wall went on seemingly straight. It was, Sarah and Lily thought, a huge city.

The trio came at last to some of the seedier parts of town. There were small huts made of rough sand bricks, some made of driftwood, and some made of shells or other debris dumped together like a shanty. Even here, there were some houses that were beautifully kept, with the wood shined and the sand swept out. Others were dirtier looking. Some had neat yards of pebbles or neatly trimmed seaweed, some had high seaweed or were just sand. Sarah thought it interesting that they had people with fewer possessions just as in her world, but even here there were some who made the most of their situations.

Finally, it started to get very dim, and the shadows were getting longer.

"We should return to the guest house," Scallop said.

Scallop waved her arm, and a carriage stopped in front of them. It was a beautiful oyster shell cracked open part way, so that one side provided a roof for them. Inside were soft pads of netting stuffed with seaweed, like pillows. On the roof sat a merman, and pulling the shell were two large rays. They climbed in and reclined on the pillows, while the shell soared across town, above several houses and buildings, and finally dove until they were on the street next to their house.

The three of them went inside and ate another meal on the balcony of their house, while Sarah and Lily watched the sun go down over the city. The sun seemed distant, as though covered by many clouds, yet the orange light of its setting painted a most beautiful picture, bathing distant buildings of coral and stone with a warm orange glow, while the deep turned blue or purple like the sky at sunset. It was a sight they would not soon forget.

Once the sun went down, the water turned not only dark but nearly black. When there was a full moon, as there would be later, they could see very dimly. With no moon, as there was that night, it was nearly pitch under the sea. The stars that appeared in the sky above the water were mere pinpoints and shed no light whatsoever under the ocean.

Scallop brought out a lamp made of some phosphorus algae in a thin container of translucent shell. Using this dim light, she walked Sarah and Lily to their rooms. There, beds of soft netting stuffed with seaweed or other soft materials awaited them. Once they were covered up, it was almost dry under the covers, although their heads lay in the warm water, and the girls could still breathe the water like it was air. They soon fell asleep, dreaming of the undersea city and wondering about the adventures that were ahead.

# 5

# Interview with King Triton

It was about mid-morning when a merman soldier arrived to inform Sarah and Lily that King Triton would expect them after lunch. That still left most of the morning for them to do with as they pleased. They spent it leisurely watching people swimming about the city, going in and out of buildings or traveling on the streets, or in some cases above them. It was a lot like watching their fish tank at home. For lunch, they ate light: fish and chips, only the chips were made of some kind of undersea plant instead of potatoes. Still, it was very good.

After lunch, Scallop led them both to the palace gate. It was, Sarah and Lily noted, a real sandcastle, only the castle appeared to be made from bricks of sand or sandstone, with pieces of shells or gems mixed in, so that it sparkled in the sunlight. In front of the gate – a raised portcullis – stood a row of mermen with the conch helmets and tridents and nets, only these wore some kind of strap over their shoulder, perhaps to denote that they were royal guards.

The girls wove their way through a series of gates, open courtyards, doors, and large chambers until the guards showed them into a large waiting room, with large plants, swaying with the tide, in the corners of the room and soft benches lining the walls. There they waited for some minutes, Scallop biding her time by swimming flips in front of the girls, who sat politely and talked quietly. Finally, a large set of double doors made of a dark, heavy wood swung open, and the old mermaid from the previous day, presumably the secretary to the king, entered.

"He will see you now," she said, turning and pausing a moment for them to follow.

They swam down a long hallway of some green stone lined with columns of sandstone. In between each column were windows made with some translucent shell as glass. Light flooded in from the sides, casting shadows along the columns. At the end of the hallway, which seemed to go on forever, they came to another set of double doors, a guard posted on either side. As they approached, one guard opened the doors.

"Triton, King of Atlanticus, Prince of the Caribbean, Keeper of the Tides, Protector of the Realm, and Guardian of the Abyss," he said as they entered.

It was a large hall, again with green stone lining the floor. Four large towers of sand formed the corners of the tall chamber, and a vaulted ceiling reached its pinnacle far over their heads. The floor ended before a raised dais at the opposite side of the room, where a large throne stood. There sat an old merman with long white hair and a beard, his hand wrapped around a golden trident, his sea green tail wrapped around the legs of the chair on which he sat. He looked exactly like every picture of Neptune the children had ever seen.

The old mermaid approached the throne and bowed. Sarah and Lily also bowed slightly – since they did not have a dress on, they could not curtsey. Scallop bowed until she did a flip.

"I am pleased to present, by your highness' own request, Princesses Sarah and Lily, Elf Friends and Maidens of Fairie, Courtesans of Queen Selena. Also, your servant, Scallop, who faced many dangers to bring them here to you."

The old man sat up slightly, moving his hoary head forward to look at them while stroking his long, white beard. He seemed at that moment very old.

"Sarah and Lily," he said slowly, "I know you are wondering why we have taken you away from your family.

We need your help in defeating a new menace, which threatens our whole community. Not ten miles from here, a great wizard is seeking to destroy us. We are asking for your assistance."

"But why do you need us?" Sarah asked. "You have all of these soldiers, and we are but little girls who cannot survive long in the water without your magic protecting us."

"It is true we have soldiers, but against this menace they are little use, for you see, the wizard, whom we have learned is named Somnambulus, lives on the beach. We cannot directly approach him, in part because he does not live in the water and in part because he uses his magic to protect himself."

"I thought that was the Sand Witch?" Lily asked, who thought again of food.

"As did we," the king continued. "You see, we did not have much information about our enemy. We only knew that many of our mermaids had been made to fall asleep and were swept out with the tide. Our people saw a woman standing on the beach one of the times this happened, but we only recently learned that she was but the consort of the wizard."

"But again, why us? Are there not many more servants who can help you? The fairies, for instance, or the sea creatures under your command?" Sarah asked.

"There are, and many of these are already engaged in the fight. But we sent for you to help with a particular set of tasks for three reasons. First, you came highly recommended. When the spell first struck our people, we reached out to our friends in the Kingdom of Fairie, and the Fairie Queen herself told us of her human friends, who happened to be at the beach at the very moment this threat arose. She told us of how you had defeated the elf witch and her goblin confederates. You seemed to be the right ally in defeating the Sand Wizard. Second, some of the tasks require someone of humankind. Our people cannot walk the beaches, and the Sand Wizard has protected his realm against any kind of magic or magical creatures by drawing a circle of protection around where he lives. It cannot keep out all magical creatures, but no one within it can work what you would call fairy magic. Third, you have inside knowledge of his home and where he lives," the mer king replied.

"How could we know about where he lives?" Sarah asked.

"You built it," he replied. "You see, he lives in your sandcastle on the very beach where you played only hours ago."

"Oh, no!" Sarah said. She felt a sudden rush of guilt, thinking that anything she had built or done had aided their enemy.

"I knew there was someone in the sandcastle!" Lily said at the same time.

"We are so sorry! We did not know that someone would move into the sandcastle," Sarah followed. "We would not have let it stand vacant so long if we had known. We have caused this disaster to come upon your lands."

"My dear children," Triton said, "It is not your fault. Who could have predicted that Somnambulus would have chosen your sandcastle, which in your world has stood such a short time, though in our time has been standing weeks? No, the issue is not how it came to be there, but how do we destroy it and him and restore balance to the natural world. For that, we have a plan, but it will require your help. Let me show you."

Triton suddenly sat up and swam off his throne with vigor, surprising Sarah and Lily a little. For such an old merman, he could move very rapidly and had greater strength than they realized. They followed him from the throne room to one of the nearby towers. They climbed or swam one after the other until they reached a spacious chamber at the top. There, in the middle of the room, sat a large globe, like a life-size snow globe, made of crystal or marble. As they approached it, he set it spinning. After a few minutes, they could see a picture within.

An image of the sandcastle appeared in the globe. On the high tower, they could see a man standing in a yellow robe gazing out over the ocean.

"Somnambulus stands ready to launch an all-out assault on the world," said Triton, "but it's the merpeople that he mainly wishes to target because we have control of the seas, where his power is weakest. He believes that if he can conquer us, it will give him an inroad into the seas. By controlling our people, he can use them to attack his enemies and rivals. But he must get us out of the way, and he has been fighting us with all the powers he has."

"If he cannot go into the sea, how will he defeat you?" Lily asked.

"He will gain control using the three tools he has," King Triton replied. "First, through actual power over the sands, he will make it dusty everywhere, darken the sun, and thereby stunt the growth of all things. He will blind those who try to approach him. He will form more and greater buildings and castles with sand, so that his troops will be protected. For you see, he can tell the sands of the earth to do what he wishes. He can form them into objects, and he can destroy any object built with or on sand. Second, he will burrow in the ground to find treasures to pay his people, or he will open gateways in the earth to bring up all manner of creatures to serve him. He can feel what is beneath the earth; vibrations in the sand flow to him like ripples in a pond. He can easily control those creatures that live in the sand. Third, he will try to put people who oppose him to sleep and invade their dreams with nightmares that make them wish to serve him. He does this by blowing sand or sleep in their eyes.

"My people have opposed his designs. We alone have stood against him when other peoples of the sea have agreed to serve him. For this reason, he has opposed us without pause. He has sent sea creatures such as crabs, clams, flounders, and octopi – those creatures that dig in the earth – to attack us. He does not control all, but enough to make it difficult for us. On land, he has other servants – people formed of sand, evil fairies, and men – so that we dare not approach the shore near his castle most of the time."

While Triton was speaking, Sarah, Lily, and Scallop saw in the globe a crab attacking a merman, and evil looking men on a boat shooting a harpoon at a mermaid diving beneath the waves. They saw a whirlwind of sand surround a fairy flying along the beach and blow her out to sea.

"Does this globe show the past, present, or future?" Sarah asked, worried about injuries to the merpeople and fairies because of these attacks.

"It mostly shows the present, what is going on in the world as seen through one of the globes that my people carry," Triton said. "These smaller globes serve as eyes to my people. It can show the past, but it is limited to what the user has seen, either personally or through his globe. It can show the future for those who have far sight, but only through great effort, and only if the user has a clear vision. I have seen the future a few times, but lately I have been too distracted by this war."

"What can we do to help?" Lily asked.

"We must destroy the sandcastle," the old merman said. "He moved into this castle, and it gives him a base from which to act. Without it, his power would not be completely gone, but it would be greatly reduced since he would have to fend for himself against the powers of nature – against wind and tide. From what we can tell, he has greatly expanded the castle and its walls and dungeons, so that his magic is tied up in their making. If they fall, he would fall, though not forever. It would, however, release those he currently controls and enable them to return to nature. He would have to work hard to regain his small kingdom."

"It is true that we built the castle and know its design and layout, but we would not know about any changes he may have made. And if his magic protects it from the tides, how can we destroy it?" Sarah asked.

"The storm that sits now off the coast could destroy it, if I could but control it. You see, the kings of Atlanticus have storm powers. We control the winds and the rains and the seas, and can make them surge and ebb. Unfortunately, mine have dwindled since a sea hag stole my trident, which served me as a focus for my energy. This is where your help is needed first," King Triton explained.

"Sea hag?" Sarah replied. "I thought you were fighting the Sand Wizard?"

"And so we are," Triton said. "We face these two enemies. You see, the sea hag, who lives far to the south, has also been making inroads into our kingdom and has captured many of our people to serve her, just as Somnambulus has. Were she to make an alliance with Somnambulus, we would have to fight on both fronts at one time. I fought with her many months ago, and I was able to banish her to the Abyss, a large hole going to the center of the earth. But in the process, she captured my trident, through which she can control those of my people that approach her realm, and she can influence the water and the tides. If you can get this back, through stealth or conflict, I can use it to destroy the castle of Somnambulus."

"You said this is where our help is needed first," Sarah said. "Where else is it needed?"

"We need you to enter the sandcastle and set free the creatures Somnambulus has imprisoned," the old merman said. "I do not wish to destroy these innocent peoples. The escape of his prisoners would also distract him from the storm, so that he would not leave, and thus it would make our destruction of his power more complete."

"Where do we start?" Lily asked.

The king explained, "First, you must go to the grotto of the sea hag and retrieve my trident. That will not be easy, for with the trident she has great powers of the sea, and she holds many of my people as slaves. Her only weakness is that she has not yet learned to use its full power. My only advice for you is to use stealth to catch her without the trident, when she is weaker. It is a long way from here, so we will have to get you closer to the entrance to the Abyss. Since you lack fins and the ability to swim underwater quickly, the fastest way to go would be on the surface by boat. We will make arrangements for your travel and find places for you to stay. Once you have the trident, you will need to return quickly to infiltrate the castle of the Sand Wizard. There is but a brief window of time while the storm tarries along the coast, so you must hurry. Once it passes, it could be many months before another storm comes, and with it another opportunity to end the power of Somnambulus."

"What about Scallop?" Lily asked. She had started to get attached to the little mermaid.

"She will come with you part of the way and be your guide," Triton replied.

"Hurray," Lily said as Scallop did a flip.

"But she cannot face the sea hag without becoming her slave, and she cannot come within the circle of protection near the sandcastle. This is my command," Triton said.

"But we are on vacation!" Sarah exclaimed. "Our parents would surely notice that we are gone for that long."

"You may have already noticed that time is passing slower here than in your land, so that should not be an issue," Scallop answered.

"Oh, you are right," Sarah said. "How else could the Sand Wizard have occupied the sandcastle for months when we only built it a few days ago?"

"Then it is settled," Triton said. "Scallop will take you back to the guest house. You should get as much rest as possible, and then we will get supplies together for you to take. You must leave on the morrow."

With that, they left the tower and the great hall, and returned to Coral, the great mer city.

# 6

# Back to the Surface

Sarah, Lily, and Scallop returned to the guest house and prepared for their trip. They spent most of the remainder of the day resting. They ate a sumptuous meal of different kinds of fish, seaweed salad, the bread-like stuff with jellyfish jelly, and a strange flavored drink, which they had to drink through a straw. Because of the sea, they could not have open containers, and both Sarah and Lily found it strange to drink while underwater. After the meal, they took a pleasant swim or walk about the neighborhood, but they did not go far, for they still had much to do, and they needed to get a full night's sleep.

Although Scallop spent most of her time with the girls, another mermaid named Bubbles joined her for part of the time. Bubbles was a perky maid with platinum blond hair. They were evidently friends and went off on occasion to talk, although Bubbles later joined the group in eating and talking. Sarah and Lily had found Scallop to be inexperienced with the world and distracted at times. Like most mermaids, she was interested in appearances, especially her own, and she did not think through the impact of her world on humans, probably because she had not known many. Yet she was very smart about the undersea world, very knowledgeable in her own right, and extremely faithful as a friend and companion. By comparison, Bubbles was not very bright at all. She was, what Scallop later called, a "water head" and did not really understand the mission or the reason for it. All that Bubbles knew was that her friend was going away, and so she was feeling a little dejected. Still, she was very friendly, and they had a pleasant afternoon.

While they were enjoying themselves, the mermen soldiers, under guidance from the old mermaid, packed for their trip. They pulled together several boxes of food, a shelter of some kind, and weapons – mostly tridents and crossbows that shot spears. Only such weapons would work underwater. They packed lightly, but because of the number of mermen in their escort, they took quite a bit more than Sarah and Lily were expecting. About dinner time, a team of young mermen carrying nothing but knives turned up and said that all the arrangements had been made. They had evidently left the city and swam many hours to prepare for travel on the surface, although they did not say exactly what those preparations were.

That evening, a black-haired merman with steely grey eyes showed up at their door.

"I am Barracuda, Captain of the Guard," he said. "I will be leading the expedition to take you as far as the Abyss. We need to discuss the plan, and if it meets your approval, we will make the final preparations for tomorrow."

Barracuda came into the guest house, followed by another merman carrying a great scroll made of some kind of fish sinew. He unrolled it on the table; it contained a large chart. Sarah and Lily looked at it anxiously. Sarah in particular loved maps. Most of her favorite books contained a small map to go along with the story, but none of the details of this map were familiar. It seemed like the map of another world, as indeed it was. Sarah found Coral on the map and recognized a few of the ridges and the little cove they had hidden in briefly, but the rest was a series of mountains and hills she did not remember seeing. One or two of the mountains ended with a large circle on the map – islands, she guessed, for they would seem as mountains with an unchartered top outside of the water. In the lower right hand corner, she saw a large crack labeled "Abyss." It was a detailed map of the ocean floor.

"Here is the plan," Barracuda explained. "We will leave tomorrow immediately after dawn. We will travel roughly due west. That is, of course, going the opposite direction, but it will only be briefly. There is a man on the docks who is friendly to the merpeople. He has a boat that we will use. Then we will travel east-southeast until we come to Mount Wood, where you can stay while we resupply. There are people there on the top. (Sarah guessed Barracuda meant Mount Wood was an island.) Then it's onward to the Misty Mountain. That will be the last stop before we dive and swim to the Abyss. We will wait outside at one of our guard towers while you continue on. At Triton's orders, we cannot enter or risk becoming slaves of the hag."

"How will you accompany us if we are in a boat?" Lily asked.

"We will be swimming just below you, helping to push the boat along," he replied. "We will be in constant contact with you."

"Will you provide us with additional instructions once we get to the Abyss?" Sarah asked. "I'm not sure we will know what to do or where to go."

"Yes, we will discuss with you the way and the best plan," he explained. "Although it has been some time since I have ventured in the Abyss, I will provide you with what map I can. We will do whatever we can to support you, short of actually entering ourselves. This is only wisdom. It would not benefit you to have our company with you if we were made to turn on you by the hag."

"How many mermen are you taking?" Sarah asked.

"An even dozen, including myself and Scallop," he said.

"Do you think that will be enough?" Lily inquired. "What if we are attacked by a shark or something?"

"It is surely enough to protect you from harm," Barracuda answered. "It is not enough men to enter into battle with the hag or the wizard, but that is not our intent. This is a mission of stealth. If we were to take many more, it would draw more attention to us and probably lead to a direct attack by our enemies. I know you may worry about what will happen to us after the king's description of our recent battles, but I can assure you that every one of these men is worth ten others. They are truly our best warriors. You will be safe."

Sarah and Lily asked several other questions about the plan, but it was well-laid, so they eventually decided to go to bed.

The next day, the expedition was off soon after the sun was up and shining on the undersea world, although this was quite a bit later than morning on the surface. The mermen had packed all of the supplies on the backs of two large manta rays, which they led by a rope of sea hemp. At first, they went rather slowly for the sake of Sarah and Lily, who although reasonably fast swimmers could not keep up with the merpeople. So they took their time, taking many rests and meals at safe spots along the way, such as in little coves or beds of seaweed. Over the course of the day, however, they finally sped up a little in anticipation of getting to their destination that day.

The group finally arrived at a large dock in the late afternoon. Sarah and Lily saw the timber piles supporting the structure as they swam up from below. It was a long fishing pier that stuck out in the calm waters of a bay, and there were several boats tied up along the quay. They all stuck their heads out of the water near one of the boats. Being late in the day, there were few people on the dock, mostly at the very end with lines in the water. About midway along the dock was a small shed, where a man sold bait and cold drinks. At the back of the shed, a little boy sat with his fishing line in the water.

"Abraham," Barracuda whispered to the boy.

"Barracuda," the boy recognized him immediately. "Where did you come from?"

"We have come a long way from our city. Did our people talk to you and your father yesterday? Is everything ready? We have need for great speed."

"Yes, it is all arranged," the boy said.

Abraham got up and poked his head in the door and spoke to the man inside. Then he closed the door and walked a little ways up the pier. He walked past motor boats, large sail boats, and expensive fishing boats to a simple row boat. It was not as fancy or as large as the others, but it looked sturdy enough. It was new, not some old rickety wooden boat, and it held both oars and a small sail and mast, which could be attached to the middle of the boat if needed, like a wind surfer. Inside the boat were two life jackets as well as fins and goggles - everything the girls had wished they had when swimming across the ocean. There were some camping supplies, including a tent, sleeping bags, a lantern, and a compass. There was also a cooler and some clothes.

Sarah and Lily swam to a ladder on the side of the dock, but before they could climb out, Scallop stopped them.

"Wait! Let me return you to your world," she said.

Scallop kissed them and brushed her tail beneath them. They noticed no difference, but she evidently removed whatever magic that allowed them to breathe underwater. Then Scallop, Barracuda, and the others dove beneath the waves out of sight.

Sarah and Lily climbed out, and then got into the boat. The little boy untied the boat and cast it off. Sarah picked up an oar and used it to push off from the dock. She rowed a few times, but noticed the boat moved much quicker than her rowing warranted, and turned even when she made no effort to turn it. She looked down into the water and saw the mermen beneath the water. They were pushing the boat. Then two of them grabbed the rope and pulled them rapidly out to sea. At first, they remained hidden until the dock was distant. They might put a head or a face above water, but nothing more than that until the entire dock was out of view.

As they sped out to sea, Sarah and Lily opened the cooler. Inside were some familiar soft drinks and sandwiches, which they devoured with relish. Although they liked some of the sea food, they had missed familiar products – those not made of fish. Also, everything in the ocean seemed to have a salty or fishy taste. They had longed for something sweet, such as the fruit that was in the cooler.

After lunch, Sarah and Lily put on the dry clothes. The sun was now starting to set, and they relaxed a bit and soaked up every last ray. No matter how much they enjoyed the beautiful undersea world, the girls had deeply missed just being able to sit in the sun and breathe the sea air. After a while, they noticed that their skin dried out, another sensation they had missed. Their skin never did get pruny underwater. It must have been something about the magic of the mermaid, yet they had missed just being dry and having on dry clothes.

As the sun went down, the mermen continued to pull the boat forward, while the girls huddled together at the bottom of the boat to get out of the wind. Although warm, the night air was cooler than they expected, and the breeze made them rather chilly. At the bottom of the boat, under the cooler, the girls found a large woolen blanket, which they used to cover themselves. They quickly fell asleep.

The girls woke up to the distant sound of a fog horn. Sarah sat up, and sure enough, a large freighter was visible, although it was still very distant, perhaps a mile or more. She wondered if the men in the ship could even see their tiny boat or them. The fact that the boat continued without stopping until waves took it out of sight made her think that they could not, for certainly they would have stopped to help a small boat so far afield in the large ocean.

The boat appeared to have stopped drifting, and the rope at the bow of the little boat hung loose, so it was not being pulled. Yet the girls did not drift very far, despite the waves. Probably the mermen had anchored the ship or prevented it from drifting somehow. Sarah looked around for the mermen, but as it was still in the dim light of early morning, she could not see them below the surface, and no one made an appearance above the waves until the ship was far out of sight and the sun was high above the horizon. Then Scallop raised her head up near their little boat.

"Is the big ship with the people gone?" the mermaid asked.

"Yes," Sarah and Lily responded together.

"Mind if I come up for a while?"

Sarah and Lily both nodded their heads.

"You had best shift your weight to the other side of the boat," Scallop said. "That's it. That way I can lean over this side. Wouldn't want to tip over the boat. Anyway, I was getting lonely. Barracuda may be a great warrior, but he is not much of a talker and not much company for a young mermaid such as I am. The others are not much better. I traveled in silence for some time, and then I fell asleep on the manta ray while they continued through the dark. They finally stopped late into the night and set up camp below. They tied the boat to a float, which is anchored to the bottom. Because of the depth, they could not tie the boat directly. I think I am the first to wake up, so I swam up to see you."

The girls and the mermaid chatted for some time. Scallop asked a lot of questions about their world, about how the boat worked, about the blanket and how it was made, and about the life jackets and other things in the boat. She was particularly interested in Sarah's description of the making of wool – how people sheared the hair of sheep and wove it together. Evidently, the merpeople had no similar process for making anything similar under the sea.

While they talked, Sarah and Lily pulled more food out of the cooler and ate breakfast – some milk, fruit, bacon, and a croissant roll each. This led to another set of questions from Scallop about their food, how they baked bread and cooked bacon, and how they milked cows. Aside from the cooking, which merpeople did not do because they could not build fires, she seemed to understand the rest of their descriptions quite well, as they milked octopi and other sea creatures, and they harvested fruit from undersea plants. Finally, Scallop excused herself and swam off to get some breakfast.

Meanwhile, Lily put on her goggles and looked below. She could see a rope dropping from the buoy nearby down to a camp about a hundred feet below them. They had stretched a tent of some kind of material, which served as a shelter from sea creatures and unkind eyes. It blended in fairly well with the bottom, and it was only with great effort that Lily could see it. She could see the manta rays, tied nearby, sleeping on the bottom, and she could see a merman swimming back and forth, evidently a sentry of some kind. The other mermen were just beginning to move about the camp, getting food out of containers stacked near the rays. Scallop swam down and opened one box, sat for a while eating, and eventually swam back up to the boat.

It was about half an hour later when the expedition set out again. The mermen packed up all of the stores, folded and put away the tent, loaded the rays, and swam back up to the surface. They then instructed Sarah and Lily about how to put up the sail, how to position it to go to a certain location, and how to tack when the wind was not blowing the direction they wanted to go. This required crisscrossing every so often and moving the sail around to catch the wind from another direction. The girls struggled at first to learn the skill. The mermen were always coming up and providing advice, but luckily they had the wind at their backs most of the time. As they continued on, Barracuda swam up and spoke to Sarah and Lily.

"We are about half way to our destination," he said. "One more full day, and we should arrive. We may have to stop briefly, however. You know that a great storm was nearing the land from which you came. We have largely gone around this storm, but I have seen some clouds gathering. We will likely run into a line of storms swinging around from the north. If so, we may have to pause and cover the boat until the weather has passed."

"Please, can you tell us a little more about the Abyss and the hag that we have to face?" Sarah asked politely. Although he was a little rough around the edges and sometimes very direct, Barracuda had warmed up to them a bit and was talking more freely.

"I do not often speak of that battle, for we lost many mermen, some to death, some to become the hag's slaves. Yet, I will this once. The Abyss is a great crack in the ocean floor that lies some miles from Coral on the very edge of King Triton's realm. It has been there as long as our records have lasted, being the result of some ancient earth tremor or lava flow. It goes very deep within the earth, many miles at least. For the most part, our people have kept away from it other than those with adventurous hearts. It contains many ancient sea creatures and evils, which we do not name, but it also contains vast treasures of jewels and metal once buried in the earth. So it has attracted many mermen, often to their deaths.

"Some years ago, when I was but a young man, the hag took up her abode there. She was old even then. Some say she was once a mermaid," Barracuda explained.

"I doubt that," said Scallop, "for she is old and ugly and fat, such as no self-respecting mermaid would become."

"There are many ancient things about which you know little, Scallop," Barracuda said. She bowed in respect.

"If she is not a mermaid," he continued, "she is related to us, for she also is half-fish in appearance. And she was friendly to the merpeople at first. At that time, her name was Sandina. She lived among us and used her magic to help us at times. For she could sometimes see the future, she had great powers of persuasion using her voice, and she had learned the innate powers of plants and animals, so that she could make powerful potions for healing, for love, and for control. After a time, she started to court the previous king, Gale III. When he spurned her, she started to challenge him, convincing other mermen that he was leading them astray through his timidity. Eventually, he banished her.

"That was more than a decade ago, and during that time, we heard little about her, although some believe that she found a home in the Abyss. From time to time, we hear tales of her. Someone would disappear and later escape, saying she had captured them. Mining parties would see her in the distance, or hunting parties would run across her. It was in one of these when I first saw her as a teen.

"Then about three years ago, our people started to run into mermen who claimed that they served only her. Hagatha, they called her. These were the dark mermen. We called them thus because of their dark, colorless hair. Though we know little about their origins, it is evident that they live far from the sun, which tans the skin and lightens the hair. They tried to dominate and attack peaceful merpeople, so King Triton sent his troops out to push them back. There were some skirmishcs, but we were generally triumphant. Then about six months or so later, a full blown war broke out. Her servants had metal helmets and breastplates, so that our tridents were ineffective. They made a lot of ground until we started using nets to entangle them. We finally forced their retreat to the edge of the Abyss.

"Hagatha's mermen made one last stand, encouraged by her very presence. During this last battle, many mermen fell. My mentor and friend, Pike, once captain of the guards, fell with a trident wound through his chest. Two of the mermen caught King Triton in a net. Although he is a powerful warrior, he is getting old, and they used this to their advantage. While he was down, before we could come to his rescue, Hagatha wrenched the trident from his hand. She did not know then how to use its powers, but, knowing that it was a great weapon, she retreated with it, leaving many of her people to die.

"To protect our realm against her people, we built several towers along the Abyss to watch for any advance and to protect against any attack. Hagatha has been able to use some of the powers of the trident, but not all. Mainly, she has learned to control mermen and force them to do her bidding, but it takes great concentration. She has only been able to make occasional attacks on the towers. We always beat back her armies, but not without losses. It is only a matter of time before we must place more guards here or risk her invading our lands. This time, with the power of the trident, she would be much more successful.

"You can see now why the Sand Wizard is such a threat. With two of our borders under attack, from the wizard and the hag, we cannot defend ourselves without allies. Their magic is too strong. Each alone would be a threat that would require our full attention. Together, our kingdom will fall. It is for this reason we need your help. But be not afraid; we will get you the help you need and deserve to face this threat," Barracuda concluded.

The expedition continued on for some hours in silence, the mermen going beneath the surface. Sarah and Lily sailed the boat, while the mermen made occasional corrections. After a time, Scallop returned alone and spoke to the girls, making jokes and laughing as was her nature. Still, the burden of their task now lay heavily on them. About mid-afternoon, the expedition ran into the storm as promised. They stopped, took down the sail, and placed a tent made of some stretchable membrane over their boat. There, they waited out the rain and wind. Lily fell asleep as they waited, but Sarah continued to think on the story of the old hag and wondered what the future would hold.

# 7

# The Sea Elves

The storm shook the boat violently for perhaps an hour. For Lily, it was like a cradle, gently rocking her to sleep. For Sarah, it jolted her awake, but she let her sister sleep. Once the storm passed, the travelers resumed their way, the mermen pulling the boat as before.

The expedition continued for many more hours until, finally, as the sun set, they reached a wooded shore. Sarah could only guess this was Wood Island, or Mountain as the mermen called it. As they continued around the isle, they came to a low, flat, sandy beach. There the mermen pushed the boat up on the shore.

"You may make a camp upon the shore, according to your people's custom," Barracuda said, his head sticking out of the shallow water. "The tent and other supplies you'll need are in the box we've left in the boat. Tomorrow, we will swim to the coral reef and restock our supplies of fish and other game and allow the manta rays to feed. Our camp will be just off shore, and we will keep a watch on your camp. If any wild animal should attack, you can run into the water to escape."

"Are there wild animals on the island?" Lily asked.

"I believe there are some, though they will not usually bother you," he answered.

The mermen left, and Sarah and Lily dragged the box onto the shore. Inside was the membrane tent, which they set up quickly as the mermen had showed them during the storm. Then they went to collect firewood. There was some driftwood that the girls had seen nearby, and then they found some dry kindling and a few branches on the edge of the woods. They were a little afraid to go very deep into the forest, especially as the sun was now behind the horizon, and it was very dark under the canopy of trees. It was almost impenetrable with so many bushes and undergrowth. But they were able to collect most of what they needed without stepping inside the tree line. With the wood in hand, they used a lighter that Abraham had left in the boat to start a fire.

With the fire burning, they were able to cook some meat – mostly bacon and a little fish provided by the mermen – and also a can of beans. It was good to finally have a hot meal after so many days without one. They drank another soft drink from their cooler and some water from a jug, which they afterwards returned to the boat. Soon, they were settled under their blanket at the front of their tent, warming their feet by the fire. The sea breeze had kicked up, so it was a cooler than it had been. At first, Lily was a little wary of wild animals, but after not seeing anything for a while and knowing that the mermen were watching them, they decided to go to sleep without setting a watch.

The girls woke up some hours later; at least it seemed so by the height of the moon in the sky. What woke Sarah was something pointed poking her brow. She opened her eyes, and there before her was a dark figure with a bow, an arrow notched, the string pulled back, and the arrowhead pointed at her temple. What woke Lily was someone talking in a foreign language. Another figure held an arrow to her head as well, but from a distance of a foot or so. The two figures spoke silently to each other from each side of the tent, although the girls could understand nothing of the language. It seemed to them as a Native American tongue, though perhaps a little less rough and halting, a little more fluid.

The girls sat up, their captors following their motions with their bows and arrows. The girls thought about the words of the mermen and looked to the ocean as a possible escape route, but there were half a dozen more figures between them and the sea, each armed to the teeth with a sword, knife, and bow. They would have never made it into the water without being intercepted or possibly killed. They decided quickly with only a look into each other's eyes that there was little chance of escape, and they raised their hands slowly, one by one.

The figures motioned with their bows and arrows for the girls to stand and move away from the tent and the water into the forest. The girls followed their captors to a previously undetected path into the forest. Once they started moving, their captors unnotched their arrows and put them back in their quivers, as though some danger were past. They walked quickly but carefully through the undergrowth, stopping often to point out the nearly invisible path to Sarah and Lily so they would not trip. The same two figures that held bows to their heads followed on either side of them to guard them.

The crew moved silently through a rain forest, composed of palms (both coconut and date), pine, bamboo, flowering bushes, ferns, the occasional cacti, and various other tropical trees and shrubs. It was a beautiful island and obviously bountiful. They seemed to go for some way, although it was hard to tell distances because of the twisting and turning they did to avoid a swamp, rocks, or other obstacles. They seemed to be making more or less for a low hill. After a few minutes, they came to a stream about thigh-high, and their hosts paused to fill their water bottles. Sarah stuck her finger in the water and then in her mouth to confirm that it was indeed fresh water. Sarah and Lily both bent down and drank a little of the water. One of the figures handed them bottles, which the girls emptied and then refilled. Although they drank from the water jug on the boat, it was neither as healthy tasting nor as cold as the water of the stream, which was cold and delicious.

Once refreshed, the girls continued through the trees toward the hill. Eventually, they started to climb, weaving back and forth from cliff to hill until they reached the top. The hill was not very high, at least judging by the time it took to climb it, but it did command an awesome view of the island and the sea. The island itself was not very large – only about two or three miles long and a mile wide. The beach where they landed and the hill were both on the southern end of the island, but on the opposite sides of the island, the beach to the southeast and the hill to the southwest. From the vantage of the hill, the girls could see theirs was the only beach of any width on the island. Across the entire south side of the island, the trees grew down to the very edge of the sea except where the hill dropped off steeply about forty or fifty feet to rocks below. They could not see the north shore of the island.

The figures escorted Sarah and Lily through the trees until they came to a large clearing, where a bon fire was burning. As they entered the clearing, the figures finally pulled back their hoods, and Sarah and Lily saw their faces in the firelight. They saw their high cheekbones, delicate features, and pointed ears. They were not men, as the sisters had supposed, but were elves! They seemed different from the other elves the girls had seen in fairyland. These had dark tan skin, as though exposed to the sun, with curly or wavy hair, generally light colored or blond. Though they were obviously elves based on their stature and features, they were not of the same tribe or line as the others Sarah and Lily had seen.

The elves escorted them to the fire. There on a throne made of bamboo sat an elf with white hair and a crown made of pink flowers. Like the others, he wore a simple sleeveless robe and bamboo sandals. He raised his hand in greeting.

"Welcome, Sarah and Lily," the elf said in English. "We have been waiting for you to come for some days now."

"You were waiting for us?" Sarah asked. "Waiting to ambush us?"

"What is this? Did they bring you here forcibly?" he asked.

"Yes," Lily said. "They woke us up, too."

The king exchanged some words with the soldiers in their own tongue and then turned back to the girls. "You will have to forgive the zeal of my people. They misunderstood my commands. We are a warlike people. What with the threats from Somnambulus and spirits from the sea, we must be constantly on our guard. My instructions were simply to bring you here, both for your own protection and so that we might speak before you continue on your journey."

"But the mermen were watching out for us," Sarah said.

"No doubt they were guarding you the best they could, but they would not be able to protect you from threats on land. Somnambulus may be a great distance from here, but he could still cast spells on you if he knew where you were. He could bury you in the sand or make giant crabs dig up from underneath you and attack. That is part of his power," the elf said.

"You are familiar with the mermen and our mission against Somnambulus?" Sarah asked.

"We are in close communication with King Triton. His envoys came to us last night, so we knew you were coming this way, although we did not know that you would stop on this island. I did not learn that until you landed, and my people saw you. Triton and I have been in communication about Somnambulus and coordinating a plan. My people talk to the mermen more than most elves, and it was through me that Triton contacted Selena and learned of you," the elf explained.

"So you are elves? But you are not like the other elves we have seen," Sarah said.

"Yes, we are what you would call sea elves. You see, the elves split into several tribes long ago. Most chose to live in the woods. A few continued to maintain the height of our culture in the Old Country. Then there were those of us who became enamored of the sea and chose to live along the coast or on islands such as this. We are not as united as the other elves, being isolated more by distance and shoreline, but we are still a great people. Unlike our brethren from the woods, we have a great understanding of ships and naval warfare. We know both the ways of the sea and of the creatures under the sea. We swim deep, and the merpeople come to us often to learn of events on the land. That is how we came to know of the threat from Somnambulus and Triton's plan to rescue, not only his people, but all people from destruction," the sea elf said.

"Are you going to help us in our mission?" Sarah asked.

"We will provide you with what help we can," he replied. "It is late, and you still have far to go. We will let you sleep before talking more. My servants will take you to a safe place where you can sleep without worry."

"But what about Scallop and the mermen?" Lily asked. "They must be worried."

"We have already told them where we were taking you, and we have left a runner on the beach in case they need to contact you about something," he said.

Some elves then escorted Sarah and Lily to the base of a large tree, and before they could say anything, a rope ladder dropped down. They looked up and could see a wooden platform hidden among the branches. It was a wonder they had not sccn any of the platforms when they approached, but neighboring palm trees leaned over them and covered them up, and the elves had camouflaged them. Sarah and Lily climbed up the ladder after one of their hosts. The platform was not large, really more of a crow's nest, except that there were no railings other than large leaves hanging down that covered the platforms. The elves, of course, did not need railings, for they were as comfortable in the trees as on the ground. The elf gave them some bedding, which they rolled out on the platform close to the trunk so they would not roll off. Luckily, Sarah and Lily were used to tree houses, having one at home, although theirs was not nearly this high off the ground. With all the commotion and the long hike, they were exhausted and fell asleep almost instantly.

The next morning, one of the sea elves took Sarah and Lily before the king once more. He had already laid a table out for them with coconuts, pineapples, mangos, and other tropical fruits and nuts. They ate heartily, even as the king continued to speak to them.

"You slept well, I trust," he said.

"Yes," they both replied.

"Good. Eat your fill, since it will likely be the last meal you eat out of water for some time. I wished to speak to you of this threat. For you see, while you accepted the mission from Triton and the mermen, the wizard Somnambulus threatens all of Fairie. His power is spreading like a dark cloud to cover all the lands. His control over things of the earth and mud challenges us all, but especially the creatures from the ground – the dwarves and gnomes. Many of these I fear he has already influenced for evil and turned them against the fairies and elves, the creatures of the air and woods. In a short time, he has raised an army and is slowly conquering our people. Many have already died. It is important that you understand that you fight for all fairy peoples and not just for the mermen. Even Queen Selena will one day fall if you are not successful," the king said.

"But how do we fight against such a power?" Sarah asked.

"Although the wizard's power is great, he is still but newly arisen. His power extends but a short way unless he expends the considerable energy required to concentrate on his remote enemies. Also, he cannot, as of yet, focus on more than one area at a time. In other words, he cannot focus on all areas surrounding him at one time. His gaze is only a single direction. The only exception is the circle of protection, but that has its limitations. There is magic that can get through that circle, although it protects from most magical creatures. Use this knowledge to your advantage. Take with you those magical objects that he will not notice. Approach him from many directions so that he is unable to protect himself against all at one time. If you do this, you will be successful."

"But what about the sea hag?" Lily asked. "Can you help us against her?"

"Unfortunately, I know little to nothing about her. She is an enemy of the merpeople. I know that she lives in a great grotto deep in the Abyss, and that she has been capturing mermen to slave for her in her mines. Our people have been unable to dive that deep. But I know that she is hungry for power, and that she is obsessed with her own beauty since rejected by one of the previous mer kings," the king said.

"We appreciate the advice and help," Sarah said.

"That is not all I can provide," he replied. "Here are some items to help. First, you may choose weapons of your very own from our armory to take with you to protect yourselves. You will need them. But I also have special gifts for each of you. For Sarah, I provide this elven cloak, which will help to hide you when you face Somnambulus."

The Elf King handed her a light blue-grey cloak that shimmered in the light, as though made of silver thread. Yet when he held it up in front of a tree, it reflected the browns and greens, making it almost invisible.

"My people make these, as do most elves, so that we may hide easily in the woods from prying human eyes. We made this one especially to hide on the seas, but it will work elsewhere. If you cast it over the top of your boat, no one can see you but will confuse you with the waves," he explained.

"Thank you," Sarah said.

"Next, for Lily, I present this potion of shrinking. You have used it once before. It will help you when it comes time to face Somnambulus, when there is no other way to come before him. You will understand when the time comes and will know when to use it," he said.

"Thank you," Lily said.

"These are wonderful gifts and all," Sarah said, "but what we really need are companions. We have been told that we must face both the hag and the wizard alone. We are but little girls, and although we are willing to do anything for our friends and trust our prayers that we will be safe, we are being asked to take on a lot of responsibility for others without any help."

"We had never intended to send you alone on such a mission. That is why we spoke to Selena and brought you someone to accompany you, who can protect you from harm and help you in making your decisions," the king said.

As he spoke, the elf lifted his hand so as to indicate in front of him. The girls both turned to look. A crowd of elves stood around them to attend to the king. At first, they thought he meant one of them, but as the king spoke, the sea elves all moved to one side or the other, making a hole between them. There, standing some ways off but approaching between the others was another elf. Only this elf was not like the sea elves. He had dark hair, with large ears and a slightly pointed nose. He looked from a distance a little like a mouse.

"Elwin!" Sarah and Lily said together as they both ran to embrace him.

# 8

# An Old Friend

"It's great to see you again," Sarah said, while Lily hugged Elwin around the middle.

"It is good to see you," Elwin replied. "Not been down any mouse holes lately, have you?"

"Not been chased by a cat, have you?" Sarah teased in return.

It was something of an inside joke. When they had first met, a witch had transformed Elwin into a mouse, and he had been living inside the walls of the witch's cottage. A cat had chased them both. After they escaped, Elwin had accompanied the girls on many of their adventures and had grown very close to them.

"When was the last time we saw each other?" Elwin asked.

"It was the Festival of the Spring Equinox, just before Daddy got home," Lily said.

"That's right," said Elwin. "You were both wearing gowns, and we danced the night away, the fairies dancing in circles around you. It was such a wonderful time. I only wish that we could have continued to see each other, but of course, I have been very busy and was gone from Fairie for some time. Have you been back to see Queen Selena much?"

"No. We have not been doing anything since Daddy got home," Lily said as they walked back to the table in front of the Elf King and sat down again.

"Please, sit and eat," the king said. "It cheers my heart to see such good friends reunited."

"We have not seen the fairies at all for the past few months. In fact, we really have not had any adventures at all, at least not until this week," Sarah continued. "We went to stay with the merpeople, and, well, you probably know all about that."

"I know that you were with merpeople and about the mission. Indeed, I was the one who brought the news. I have been here for more than a week. You see, since my rescue from the witch and our victory in the Battle of Goblin Hall, Queen Selena has asked me to serve as an ambassador to other fairy peoples. I have traveled about quite a bit, and so was gone from Fairie for most of the year," Elwin explained.

"Wow!" said Sarah. "You must tell us of your travels."

"Mostly, I have been visiting the Emerald Isle across the sea, trying to forge a treaty with the leprechauns. They were once the traditional allies of the fairies, but you see, we have not been in close contact since our people migrated to the New World. I also spent several months in the desert trying to negotiate release of some of our people being held by Quetzalcoatl, a Native American spirit. While the humans resolved many of their differences with the natives long ago, there still remain many conflicts in fairyland, although I believe we made some real progress in our relationship.

"I had only just gotten back from the lands to the South, when we received a message that the Sand Wizard had been attacking the merpeople. We had known of the Sand Wizard for some months, at least according to our time. He has been building up his power base and was finally making his move against the fairy peoples of the sea. The queen dispatched me at once to bring the news that you were in the area and for King Triton to contact you at once. Because I had never been to the ocean and knew of no way to get in touch with the merpeople, I came here to the sea elves. Of course, we knew all about our cousins, though I had never been here, and we knew that they were in close contact with King Triton. So I came here with the message. I have received several sprite messengers since then, bringing me updates. I had, of course, hoped that you would come here, but no one knew exactly where you were or the course you were taking. When I awoke this morning, I was told I was wanted by the king, and, lo, here you are as well," Elwin said.

"So will you be coming with us on our adventure?" Lily asked.

"My instructions were rather broad. I am to advise the merpeople and help them in any way I can. I can think of nothing I would like better than to learn more about the sea and to help you in your endeavors, with the king's permission, of course," Elwin said.

"This has been my intention all along," the king replied. "We wished to send someone with you to assist you in your journeys. But our tribe is small, too small to give up a member who is not really much help other than having some knowledge of boats. Elwin, however, seems to be very interested in going, so he can represent the elves in this affair."

"You see, as I just mentioned, I had never seen the ocean," Elwin continued. "Now that I have, I am intrigued and want to learn as much as I can about the underwater world. It is really quite beautiful, and the sound of the waves crashing is entrancing. I would not mind staying longer with my cousins, perhaps even becoming a permanent ambassador here so that I can make a longer study and perhaps spread the word of the beauty of this place, its freedom and easy living. Most of my people know little or nothing about the sea. Not since we crossed over some centuries ago have we been here because of the great distance. Some have gained a fear of the sea, but I wish to correct that."

"That will have to wait until Somnambulus is defeated, if at all," the king said. "Right now, you should probably prepare for the remainder of your mission. By now, the mermen are hard at work replenishing their stock of fish. They will be ready to leave after lunch. You should finish packing your goods back into your boat and be prepared to depart this afternoon."

The girls and Elwin finished their breakfast, after which the elves provided them each with a dagger, a wetsuit made of some kind of protective coat, which the elves said was hardened by sap, and a metal crossbow made for firing underwater. Then some of the sea elves guided them back to the beach. It seemed a much shorter march than the night before, although this may have been because they took a more direct route back. When they got to the beach, the boat had floated many yards off shore as the tide had come in. Several of the sea elves dove into the water to get the boat back, swimming expertly. Suddenly, Scallop popped her head out of the sea. The elves and Scallop conversed for a few minutes, although Sarah and Lily could hear nothing over the waves. Then she waved at them on the beach and dove. The elves returned with the boat a few minutes later.

"The mermen kept the boat from floating away. They say they will be back after lunch to get you and the boat," one of the sea elves said.

Sarah, Lily, and Elwin nodded and started to take down the camp site. They packed up the tent, the blankets, and the food, and placed them in the boat. The elves, meanwhile, provided a store of dried fruit and nuts for them to take, along with coconut milk and a strong drink made of an herb – something similar to tea but with a grassy flavor. They were grateful since they were not looking forward at all to fish sustenance. They packed it all neatly in the boat, which they tied to a tree near the shore to make sure it didn't wander off again. Then Sarah and Lily went inland a ways to a secluded spot on the stream so they could take a bath, while Elwin retuned to the elf village. The girls finished washing and drying out their clothes in the hot sun, and then dressed and returned to the village for lunch. A dinner that included a salad and a cooked waterfowl hit the spot. They wanted to enjoy cooked food while they could. They packed up the leftovers in the cooler to take with them. Once they finished their meal, they returned to the beach with the king and his entourage.

"I must stress at our parting how grave the task is that faces you," the king said. "The Sand Wizard is a threat to all fairy peoples. We need your help once again to save our people. While you are very small, you have an internal strength, some power that God has given you alone. I can see it from looking at your spirits. Use this power. Rely on your inner strength, and you will be able to overcome the evil of the wizard. Do not try to face him alone, but rely on your friends. There is even greater strength in friendship. We will remember your deeds in stories and song. Now, you must be on your way – to the end of your quest, and then follow the sun westward home."

"Westward home!" all of the sea elves shouted.

Sarah, Lily, and Elwin loaded in the boat, and the Elf King waved at them as they launched from the shore using the paddle in the boat. It took a bit of rowing to get them past the waves. Once they were past the breakers, however, the mermen grabbed the rope and pulled them out to sea. They turned back to the king, who was now small upon the beach. They waved back to him one last time, as he turned and marched into the interior of the island.

Once they were away from the pull of the island, Scallop and Barracuda stuck their heads above water near the boat.

"Are you ready to move on?" Barracuda asked. The girls nodded.

"Who is this stranger?" Scallop asked. They introduced Elwin and explained how they knew him.

"This is well," Scallop said. "I know it was going to be difficult going into the wizard's castle alone. I don't know that I could do it, but having friends around always helps."

"Is this our last stop?" Lily asked.

"No. We have one more stop," Barracuda said. "We are trying to get as close as we can on the surface before diving. Then we will have to dive and swim some way on the bottom of the ocean through a lot of obstacles. We will take a wide berth and approach the Abyss from the south. That way, the hag's spies are less likely to detect us coming."

The expedition continued on the rest of that day. Sarah and Lily sailed the boat, and Scallop popped her head above water from time to time to chat. Elwin and Scallop got along famously at once. He asked her about life underwater, about the sea creatures and fish, about the tides and waves, and about the geography of the ocean floor. Scallop asked him about life in the Kingdom of Fairie, about Selena and her family, and about life among the fairies. Sarah and Lily joined in when they had some tidbit of history to add, but they mostly listened.

The friends passed the day without event until the sunset. Then they stretched the canvas over their boat to make a little tent floating on the water. The mermen must have camped far below, since they were now entering the deeper parts of the continental shelf, but they tied the rope to one of the manta rays, who made sure the boat did not float off far from their campsite. The mermen kept watch over the girls, with one of the mermen swimming just below the surface and popping his head up from time to time to check on them.

Although they could not make a fire to cook with, the three did light a lantern and sat up eating their dinner and talking. It was just like the good times they had spent together long ago, although certainly being stranded in a boat was different than tramping through the woods. And of course, this time Elwin was not a mouse. Eventually, Sarah drifted off to sleep, but Lily and Elwin stayed up talking late into the night. Lily had always had a connection with Elwin, especially when he had been a mouse, probably because he was soft and cuddly. She had always wanted to rub his fur, although she knew that it would offend him. Still, she always doted on him, and he returned the affection. Finally, after the moon was high, they, too, dropped off to sleep.

The next morning, the three of them woke with the sunlight and dropped their tent. Soon, the mermen were up near the surface and ready to go again. The group travelled the rest of that day far into the afternoon, stopping to rest only for meals. These were mostly pleasant affairs. They still had a lot of the elven food left, which they ate without worry, and they had the pleasant tea the elves had provided. The only thing they wished they had was a fire to heat the meat. Once meals were over, the journey continued across miles and miles of flat ocean reflecting a bright sun. They always felt out in the open, as though they were being watched, but there was nothing they could really do about it.

By the afternoon, the expedition entered into a fog bank. Although they were glad it hid their movements from prying eyes, the fog was cold and wet and left the girls shivering in the boat, even after covering with the blanket. It was more comfortable in the warm ocean water, so Sarah and Lily took turns diving into the water and swimming around with Scallop. Elwin said that he would watch the boat since he was not as cold, so both girls swam for some of the way as they traveled in the boat. Eventually, though, they grew tired and climbed back into the boat and wrapped up in the blanket the best they could.

As they continued, the fog got deeper until they reached a rocky shore, on which waves were constantly breaking. They followed the shoreline around the island until they came to a shallow bay. There, a long bamboo pier stuck out into the water. The mermen pushed the boat up to the pier and threw the rope onto the boat, which Elwin tied to a post. The girls climbed out onto the pier.

"Do not wander far inland," Barracuda instructed them. "Our people have not thoroughly explored this mountain, as it is almost always engulfed in mist. You should set up your tent close to the pier and get some rest. We will be diving deep tomorrow, and you will need your strength."

"Where did the pier come from?" Elwin asked.

"It has been here as long as I know," Barracuda replied. "There is little doubt that people once lived here, for there are buildings up on the rocks near the peak of the mountain. But we have never seen anyone here, so we believe the settlement has long been abandoned. Yet there is some magic here. The island is never without mist upon it, and it is easy to get lost here. That is why we have not explored it, and why I say again, do not leave the beach. We will come again for you in the morning."

Elwin, Sarah, and Lily walked to the shore and found a flat spot below the pier and near to the waterline at high tide. They then set up their tent and gathered some driftwood for a fire. They cooked and ate the last of the meat they had – a little of the waterfowl the elves provided wrapped in some bacon – since they knew they could not take it with them under the water. At first, they stayed up talking for a while.

"What is it like, swimming under the water?" Elwin asked.

"Well, the swimming part is just like it is when you dive in a pond or river," Sarah said, who loved to swim deep and hold her breath when they went to the pool. "When we went to the mer city, the real differences were breathing and performing ordinary tasks underwater. The breathing was much like above the surface, which felt unusual. Not sure what the mermaid did, whether we grew gills or whether it was just some magical way to allow us to breathe in the water. We had no air bubble and did not breathe air. The water seemed to fill our lungs just like air, yet we did not drown."

"What do you mean by ordinary tasks?" he asked.

"I mean the kinds of things you would do out of water and never think about doing in the water. For example, drinking and eating are very strange underwater because of the mechanics. It is hard to get something into your mouth without the sea water mixing with it, which gives everything a salty taste. Vision is somewhat blurred, and estimating distances is hard. It is a bit dimmer and harder to see, so you cannot navigate as easily as on the surface. Walking around is difficult because you are buoyant. We mostly swim, but there were times when we walked, and you bounced a lot. It was almost like what you see about people walking on the moon. Sleeping is unusual because you tend to float. They use a sort of bag to keep you from floating away. It was a little hard getting used to it."

"And of course their covers are not warm and snuggly like at home because you are wet," Lily added.

Lily stood up and looked inland deep into the mist.

"I wonder what is on the rest of the island," Lily said out loud. "If there were people here once, there must be ruins or something. We could go explore them in the morning."

"Best not to wander off," Elwin said. "Besides, we have a mission and should focus on that. We will be diving in the morning. If you really want to see, we could come back later sometime."

Lily nodded, but continued to look around whenever conversation drifted, as though she were thinking about the ruins. Finally, after chatting about their adventures for several more minutes, they fell asleep.

# 9

# The Island of Mist

That night, Lily woke when she heard footsteps in the sand and rocks outside of the tent. She sat up and looked around, but Sarah and Elwin were still fast asleep. Picking up her lantern, she looked out of the tent, but saw only the mist and a dim shadow of the pier. At first, she did not leave the tent because of fears that it might be some monster or evil man, but her curiosity got the best of her. If the people who made the noise were evil, they would have attacked them in their sleep. She wondered if they were natives or perhaps some remnant of the ancient peoples that Barracuda mentioned. Perhaps they could help their expedition.

Lily got out of the tent and peered back toward the island. She saw nothing there. She wondered if she should wake the others, but decided against it since she had found nothing. They would only complain if there was no one actually there. She wandered up and down the beach for a little ways, always keeping the tent within sight, and she tried to peer into the interior of the island, but the mist was too thick. On the way back, she came across some footprints. When she examined them, it was clear that they were not those of an animal but a biped, and that the feet were shod. There was someone or something walking near them in the mist, but it was not a native. The footprints seemed to come down the beach and then cut into the trees next to the tent.

The words came back to her about there being some kind of magic associated with the island. Thinking that maybe there was an elf or fairy watching them, Lily followed the footsteps through the mist, hoping to catch a glimpse of a fairy again, for she missed the fairy people greatly. She also had at the back of her mind the thought of exploring the ruins, although she knew that this was the wrong decision. But once she had something in her mind, it was hard for her to let it drop, and she continually thought about it and nagged other people.

Lily walked slowly, following the footprints. She passed shadows of trees, bushes, and a lot of bamboo as she hiked through a small forest and up a rocky slope until she finally came to a building, dark and ominous before her. Perhaps this was part of the ruins she wanted to see. The fog remained very thick, so that she could not make out how large the building was, but it seemed strangely shaped, with the walls at weird angles. It was just the type of building that some ancient culture might build, as the design was definitely not modern. The footprints seemed to go straight up to a wall, but she could just make out the posts of a door, evidently made of the same stone as the walls. She did not see a handle or any way of opening the door. She tried knocking, and she tried getting her hands inside the door crack to pull it open, but all to no effect. She was standing before the stone door, wondering what to do, when it suddenly flew open. A golden light spewed out, painting her and all the ground around her a light yellow. A shadowy figure stood in the doorway.

"Hello," Lily started to say, and then the light fell on the face of the stranger, and she screamed.

Back at the tent, Sarah and Elwin woke up. Elwin thought that he had heard something, and Sarah seemed to sense that something bad had happened, but neither could say exactly what it was that brought them out of their deep sleep. Then they looked around and noticed that Lily was missing.

"She must not have been gone long," Sarah said. "Her bed is still warm."

Sarah ran to the beach, and a merman stuck his head above water and swam partially on the beach.

"Did you see where my sister went?" she asked.

"No, I did not see her leave," he said. "The mist is very thick, and I did not hear anything over the waves. Is she gone?"

"Yes," Sarah replied.

"Look at these footprints," Elwin said from the other side of the tent, pointing his lantern toward the ground. Sure enough, there were two sets of footprints leading away from the campsite. The first set was a man's print, a large booted foot. The second looked like Lily's bare foot. They both led into the interior of the island.

"Lily!" Sarah called repeatedly, listening for an answer. When she heard nothing in response but the tide, she started getting upset. "Someone has her."

"Not necessarily," Elwin said. "Some of the smaller footprints are inside the large ones – in other words, the person who made them was walking behind the ones in the booted foot."

"So she is following the other? Why would she wander off after someone without telling anyone? It is so foolish. Does she not know we would worry?" Sarah asked.

"We should probably follow as well," Elwin said. "She may still be in danger if discovered."

They started down the beach where the footprints led and headed toward the tree line, when the merman called out, "Barracuda said not to go into the interior of the island. We do not know what this danger is."

"I can't let my sister go off alone. Barracuda will have to understand," Sarah said.

"I had better tell him," the merman said as he swam off.

Sarah and Elwin then took off after the trail. They followed the footprints across the island. They seemed to make a more or less straight line toward the hill at the interior of the island. They cut through the trees and came unto the base of the hill, which seemed more like a pile of rocks. The footprints followed a path up the rocks and ended before a stone building. As with Lily before them, they followed the prints straight to a stone door. There was no bell, no handle, and no way of knocking without hurting your hand.

"Perhaps we could force the door open," Elwin suggested. He pulled out his dagger and slid it into the crack between the door and the doorpost. He tried to pry the door open, but with no luck. "There must be a catch somewhere."

Then without warning, the door opened again. The light spilled out, and a figure stepped out into the moonlight. When the light struck the face, Sarah started to scream, but was too scared.

Standing before them was a man-sized figure. He was dressed as a man, with a long coat, pants, and heavy boots. His head was bald, slightly pointed, and of a ruddy red color. His eyes were somewhat larger than was normal for his proportions, and they were a little more on the side of his head than normal, at least it seemed so to Sarah. But he had little or no nose or mouth. At first, she thought he had a beard, but then she noticed the beard was moving. It was, in fact, eight tentacles growing out of his chin, if you could call it a chin. Below the beard of tentacles was his mouth, like a beak. His entire head was nothing but a squid attached to or replacing the face of a man. He reached out his hands toward them, and on each finger there were three or four suction cups, like a tentacle but without the writhing movement.

Sarah's eyes grew larger and larger, and she backed up away from the hideous countenance, when a small figure darted around the man and grabbed her. Sarah snapped out of what was sure to be a fainting spell to see that it was Lily.

"Lily! Are you OK?" Elwin asked.

"I am fine. Sarah, it is OK. I am OK," she said, shaking Sarah's shoulders to keep her alert. "I met a friend. Meet Captain Ishmael." Then she added in a low whisper in Sarah's ear, "Do not stare at him. You will hurt his feelings."

"You will excuse me if I do not shake your hand," Ishmael said in a low, gurgling sort of voice.

"Completely understandable," said Elwin.

"Nice to meet you," Sarah said, still a little confused and frightened.

"Well, come in, come in. Any friend of Lily's is a friend of mine," Ishmael said.

They passed through the door, and Ishmael shut it behind them. He led them through several passages into a large kitchen with a table and several chairs.

"May I offer you some soup?" Ishmael asked them.

"That would be nice," Elwin said.

The man poured them soup into wooden bowls and set them before Sarah and Elwin on the table with a spoon. They sat and started to eat. It was some kind of clam or crab chowder, not one of Sarah's favorite soups normally, but it was very warm and creamy and quite good after the cold night air.

Ishmael sat down at the head of the table as they ate. He and Lily had evidently already eaten, judging from their empty bowls. "I was just asking Lily how she came to be here when you walked up to my door."

"We are on a journey," Lily started.

"We came here with some friends," Sarah interrupted.

"But all I saw was you three and a very small boat tied to the pier," he responded.

"Yes, we were the only ones that came ashore. The rest are waiting for us," Sarah replied.

"But I saw no other ship," Ishmael stated.

"You wouldn't," Lily said.

"Because of the fog," Sarah interrupted. She knew she was not telling the truth, but she did not want to let on that they were alone in case this Ishmael wanted to attack them; and they did not want to provide him any information about their task in case he was an enemy.

"So what is your story? How did you come to be on this deserted island?" Sarah asked him, trying to change the subject so as not to have to discuss their own mission.

"It is a long tale, and a sad one. No doubt you are wondering about my appearance and my captivity on the island," Ishmael said.

"And also about the buildings and how they came to be here," Lily added.

"I was the captain of a ship, the *SS Handley*, which sailed in these waters. One day I met a most beautiful mermaid. I tried to convince my shipmates and several businessmen. Most, however, thought I had lost my mind. No one ever saw her but me. The ridicule I faced was almost more than I could bear, so I went away to search for the mermaid," Ishmael said.

"Was your name James Hugh?" Sarah asked, remembering the story of the old fisherman.

"As a matter of fact, yes. I had changed it to Ishmael when I left so as to hide my identity. So many ridiculed me, I could not find work under the name Hugh. How did you know?" he asked.

"We met an old shipmate of yours at a museum on shore a few days ago," Sarah said. "We never learned his name."

"Probably Brian Jakes. He was a good shipmate and one of the few who believed me. Anyway, under a new identity, I outfitted a small vessel with a handful of crewmembers so I could search for her. They knew of my mission, but I paid them well. We tried our hand at being merchantmen, but it always seemed to interfere with my searches, so I turned to piracy so I would not have to go far from the area where I last saw her. I am ashamed of my actions, but it was the only way that I could continue the search. My crew members thought that I used the mermaid story and supposed insanity as a ruse for the piracy. Little did they know it was the other way around, that I was really acting like a pirate to find the mermaid.

"Finally," he continued, "after many years of searching, I found my mermaid again. She convinced me to live with her in the water, so I dove under the waves, leaving my shipmates to think I was dead. She took me to a grotto deep beneath the waves, but when she presented herself to me, she was old and no longer beautiful. She had hidden her image in order to beguile me. When I refused her because of her lies, she tricked me into drinking a potion that transformed my countenance into the hideous figure you see. I did not drink it all. I think she was trying to turn me wholly into a creature of the deep, but I drank enough that it changed my appearance."

"It's not that bad," said Sarah, who was growing accustomed to her host's face. Although it was a little shocking at first, in fact she could still see the humanity in his eyes, and he obviously remained good at heart. She found herself being convinced by his demeanor that he wanted to help them.

"But how did you get on this island?" Lily asked.

"After she changed me, I could not bear the company of others. The witch decided to keep me hostage rather than killing me or setting me free. So she found this island, which was once the home of some ancient peoples who lived in stone houses such as this, and then she made it where it was always covered by mist. That way, no one would know I was here, and they need not see me unless I reveal myself to them. She comes back from time to time, mainly to taunt me. For a long time, I wanted to end it all, and then I wanted to get revenge, I hated the old mermaid so. It has only been in the last few years that I have come to accept my fate and make the best of my situation. Being alone gives you a lot of time to reflect on your life and the decisions you have made."

"Do you think this is the same hag that we must now face?" Sarah asked Elwin and Lily.

"His story is very similar to the one you told me," Elwin said.

"Who is this sea hag?" Ishmael asked. After they told him the tale of how they must face a great merwitch, he seemed to agree. "The pattern of her behavior and the general time frame seem to match mine. Too bad you cannot describe her or the grotto. Then I would know for sure."

"The mermen would know," Lily said.

"The mermen!" Sarah said. "Quick! Come with us to the shore. We must tell our friends we are OK. When we left, they believed we were in danger."

They ran out the door, down the hill, and through the forest back to the pier. Sarah and Lily waded out into the ocean, and there was Scallop and Barracuda, as well as several of the others, waiting for them anxiously.

"Please forgive us," Sarah said. "We chased after Lily and met this Captain Ishmael. We have been talking to him. I believe he is our friend, for he is also an enemy of the hag."

"Pleased to meet you," Barracuda said, pushing himself up with a wave using his trident and holding out his hand. Ishmael waded out quickly and took his hand.

"Tell me of this hag. What does she look like, and where does she live?" Ishmael asked.

"She is an old, slightly fat mermaid with a broad nose and gray hair. She lives in a cave below the Abyss, a great crack in the ocean floor leading to a deep that goes on for many miles."

"There can no longer be any doubt that this is the same person who enchanted me," Ishmael said. "For she lived in this same place and was as you described her."

"What should we do?" Sarah asked.

"Let me give some thought. In the meantime, there is no reason for you to stay in a tent on the beach. Come with me back to my house, and I will give you rooms. The mermen have no reason to fear. I will make sure you return to the beach first thing in the morning."

They all agreed, and Sarah and Lily followed Ishmael back to his house, where they found warm beds waiting for them – the first in which they had slept in a week. They dozed off to the sound of the ocean pounding on the beach, which, despite its distance, could be heard throughout the island. In a matter of minutes, they were sound asleep. Sarah dreamed of the sea hag and Ishmael, but Lily dreamed of the merpeople and swimming in the ocean again.

The next morning, they woke early to the sound of sea gulls crying. A bright light shone through broad open windows far overhead – it was from these that the sounds of the ocean came. They got up and dressed. Ishmael was already up, fixing sea gull eggs and kippers, a specially prepared fish. They tried them and found them pretty good, and they especially enjoyed the eggs, though they were not the same as the chicken eggs they were used to eating.

"It is a fine house," Elwin commented as they ate. "There is something elven about it. I wonder if the peoples who lived here long ago were my kin."

"I suppose it is possible," Ishmael said. "There were no records that I have found, no writing on any of the walls of this house. It appears to have been abandoned some time ago, several hundred years at least. I had always assumed they were men, but it does seem highly unusual that natives from this region would have built a house of stone."

"Our people were building stone houses and castles in these lands six hundred years ago, when they first came over with man," Elwin replied. As they ate, he described some of the architectural features that he found in common with elven buildings, which led to a discussion of castle-building and architecture in general. Sarah found the conversation very interesting, as she was interested in all things Medieval and had read several histories of the fairies.

After breakfast, Sarah asked Ishmael, "Have you given any more thought to how you can help us? We really wish to help you, and I think if she were to die, you would return to your normal self."

"Yes, I have been thinking most of the night. I have tried to remember something, some little habit or quirk, some weakness you can exploit, but not a lot stands out in my mind. She is obviously very vain, and that may be something you can use. She was always concerned with her looks and uses magic to make herself more appealing. She was always looking at mirrors. They were all over her hall.

"Another point to consider is that most of her magic comes through potions or mixtures, not from incantations or charms," he continued. "I would beware of eating and drinking anything, or even taking anything from her that might have been poisoned. That was how she tricked me. You can usually taste the potions when in food, though, because most of the ingredients come from vile things. Even eating a little can work the magic, but the effect grows with the amount you eat, so if you taste something bad from any food that anyone in her influence gives you, spit it out.

"You should also probably know that she has a lot of mermen working for her, most unwillingly. She has them digging in mines all throughout the caves near her grotto. Her guards are mostly willing servants and are not under her spell, although they obviously are taken with her and obey her. It's the workers, servants, and slaves that she has under her control. They obey, but only because she has some power over them. Among them are many other merpeoples. If you could find a way to release them from her power, they would rise up against her, but I do not know how she is controlling them. That is about all I can offer as far as help, although if there is anything else I can do, please let me know," Ishmael concluded.

They finished their breakfast in silence and rested a moment in that peaceful house. Ishmael smoked a pipe for a few minutes by the fire, while Sarah and Lily sat talking quietly. After a few minutes, the girls got up from the table and returned to their rooms to get their things together. A few minutes later, Sarah returned.

"I suppose we should return to the mermen to complete the journey," she said reluctantly. She had grown attached to their strange host and his wonderful house.

"I will take you," he replied.

"Perhaps we can come back once we are finished with our mission," Sarah said.

"Perhaps," he replied, "Although I am not sure how long this island will stay hidden once the spell of the hag is broken. I fear that a great many things will change, myself among them."

The group picked up their things and made the long walk down to the beach, where Scallop and Barracuda were waiting for them.

# 10

## The Bermuda Triangle

Sarah, Lily, Elwin, and Ishmael returned to the small pier on the Island of Mist. The sun was now just above the horizon and turned the white mist about them a golden color. They walked down the end of the pier to where their boat was, and there the mermen were waiting for them, their heads above water.

"You must leave the boat now and take to the deep ocean," Barracuda told them.

"What should we do with the boat and our supplies?" Sarah asked.

"You may leave them here safely," Ishmael told them. "I will see to it that no one disturbs them until you or the merpeople come back for them."

"You should take only your weapons, your swimming aids, and whatever supplies you wish to take in these bags," Barracuda said, handing them shoulder satchels.

They spent a few minutes getting dressed in the elven wetsuits, strapping on their daggers, and putting on the swimming fins they found at the bottom of the boat. Barracuda showed them each how to work the crossbows. These were easy to reload using a spring-loaded lever, and he told them how to point and pull the trigger. Such weapons were highly effective in the water, much more so than firearms or even traditional swords or bows still used by other fairy peoples.

They then pulled together some personal items – Scallop insisted that they each take a brush and some soap – and they put their gifts from the Elven King in their bags. They also put some of the tea and fruits and nuts in water proof bags for snacks, although most of the excess foodstuffs the mermen packed among their own. Luckily, they had little or no food that could spoil, such as meat.

They turned to dive off the end of the pier, and Ishmael said, "Good luck!" Sarah and Lily turned and gave him a hug. It seemed to take him a little by surprise, perhaps from lack of contact with other people for so long. He hugged them back. It was a little surprising to see his rough and somewhat sad visage melt into what Sarah could only describe as a smile.

The girls turned and joined Elwin on the edge of the pier, and then they jumped off the end of the pier next to where Scallop and Barracuda were swimming. In a few seconds they were underwater, and Scallop again kissed each of them, while Barracuda swam around them. The tension on their lungs lessened until they found they could breathe normally. They swam out of the little bay and headed for deeper water. Sarah found that with the flippers she could keep up better with the mermen, and they made much better time.

Once they got past the shallow waters near the island, they turned south and then dove deeper to the bottom of the continental shelf. They swam down though a layer of warm water, brightly lit by the morning sun and populated by many sea creatures. They saw dolphins, fish, jellyfish, and even a distant whale. The bright sun became more distant and the water a darker azure as they got deeper, but it was still fairly bright as they followed the bottom of the continental shelf. Despite being several hundred feet below the surface, they had not reached the drop off or the depths beyond, where the true ocean floor was. There were many plants growing in that region near the bottom of the sandy shelf. According to Scallop, they were still some miles from the drop off, as the continental shelf skirted numerous islands before they finally entered open water.

The troop swam along the bottom, past rocks, coral, and seaweed of various types. They saw a school of minnows darting among the weeds. They even saw an octopus moving along the ocean floor away from them, dropping a curtain of ink to mask its movements. It fled under a pile of rocks where its den was. Finally, they came to a large column of rocks that seemed to mark the end of a gentle slope from the island to the bottom of the shelf. There, a wide underwater plain stretched before them dotted with seaweeds, anemones, urchins, and other creatures among low flat rocks and sand.

"We must be careful here in the open," Barracuda said. "The hag's spies watch this area carefully, and they come here often. We will have to move with stealth, stealing from one rock or seaweed bed to another. Elwin and I will go first to find a path. Sarah, Lily, and Scallop will come next. The rest will come after us in twos or threes, with the two manta rays and supplies coming up the rear led by a merman apiece. While moving, do not stop. And make as little noise as possible. We must avoid attracting attention to our movements."

They started their slow, careful movements across the plain. Barracuda, Elwin, and another merman soldier would slip carefully to a bed of seaweed. When the girls and Scallop arrived in the bed, they would immediately dart to a rock or hollow. Once they left, the next group of mermen came behind to the seaweed. Then the girls would follow Barracuda to the next stop. It was long, boring work. With minimal talking, they could not socialize. It was swimming, which the girls enjoyed, but they always moved quickly and with a purpose, never leisurely or playfully. Sarah understood that they were at war, but Lily and Scallop seemed to become quickly frustrated and exhausted.

After some hundred yards of moving among rocks and plants, they came to several manmade objects on the ocean floor. First was a large jet plane. It looked old, like the kind of plane that was popular in the 1950s. It had definitely been there a long time, as it was rusted and covered with some climbing vine and with barnacles. It sat perfectly level on its landing gears, as though someone had simply landed it there. They swam under the shadow of its wings and on to the next bed of rocks.

Next was a small ship of some kind, a little newer, but still broken and decaying. It sat listed on its side, a large hole showing through its hull. They swam through the hole. Not much was left of the remainder of the boat, but debris was scattered for some dozen yards – boxes, bottles, an oar, and finally the skeleton of a man, half buried in the sand. Sarah and Lily looked the other way as they continued to swim past it. It appeared to be a small pleasure cruise ship that had gone down in a storm.

In the distance they saw other objects. There was a biplane, a fancy yacht slightly out of kilter, another jet pointed nose down into the sand, an old steamship from the nineteenth century with its paddlewheel sticking up into the air, a small World War I-era submarine half-buried in the sand, and even a wooden ship that seemed much older, perhaps a pirate ship from the eighteenth century. They were each in various stages of decay. Some seemed relatively new. Others were mostly empty shells, covered with barnacles. Yet all were damaged in some fashion.

Finally, they came to a large cargo barge, now sitting sideways with one end stuck in a pile of rocks. Barracuda swam into the interior of the barge through the hold, followed by Elwin, the girls, Scallop, and the others. It was dim inside, but they could make out piles of crates and boxes. It was otherwise unoccupied.

"We can rest here and eat breakfast," Barracuda said.

The others soon joined them, and they found seats on different-sized boxes and laid out their lunch on a large crate like a table. The mermaids ate various fish as usual.

The girls and Elwin ate mostly the nuts and dried fruit the elves had given them.

"What is this place?" Sarah asked as she started to eat.

"We are in the middle of the Bermuda Triangle," Scallop answered. "All of these planes and ships were lost over many years. They got lost in the fogs, could not find their way because of instruments going crazy, and finally sank or crashed into the ocean. It is a very common occurrence throughout this area."

"A fisherman was telling us about the triangle, but I never dreamed that it would be so bad. What is the cause of such devastation?" Sarah replied.

"Some say there is a lodestone or magnetic deposit buried far under the region that makes compasses and electronic equipment quit working," Barracuda said. "Others say it is due to weather patterns, that the winds and fogs confuse people. Then there are those who blame it on the mermaids or other sea creatures."

Sarah pulled out the compass, which she had taken from the boat. The needle was spinning around randomly. She could see how someone might get lost, especially in bad weather. She held it up for Barracuda to see.

"Yes. The effect is very real, but it is obvious that it is a combination of all of the factors. Creatures in the sea could not affect men in flying machines, so some of it must be because of weather or magnetism. Yet it is undeniable that merpeople have attacked men who survived the crashes. I have seen myself merpeople try to sink ships or drown men in the seas above us. I have also seen sea serpents wrap around a ship and squeeze it until it came apart at the seams. There are things stranger than mermaids in this sea, and a lot of creatures visit this area in particular because of the Gulf Stream, the shallowness of the water, and the relative scarcity of human contact."

"Why would mermen attack ships?" Lily asked.

"As we noted, this is enemy territory, from here to the drop off," Barracuda said. "Our people do not attack humans, although some maids often drown men out of ignorance. Rather, these are the people of the sea hag. She is the one who is directing attacks on men. Perhaps it is because of what happened with Captain Ishmael. Who knows? All creatures seem to react emotionally to pain. All I know is that she hates mankind almost as much as she hates our people."

After they ate, the troop continued on their way, moving silently from ship to plane and from rock to rock. After they had gone another half an hour, Barracuda suddenly hushed them, waving his arms for them to seek cover. The girls and Scallop ducked into a bed of seaweed. The other mermen hid among the rocks or inside old ships.

Far overhead, Sarah and Lily saw three mermen swimming toward the surface. They were similar in stature to the other mermen the girls had seen, only they had pale skin and dark hair, as though it had been a long time since they had been on the surface or in the sunlight. They swam toward something on the surface. At first, they could not see what it was, but then Sarah recognized the spade-shaped bottom of some boat. It was a small craft, perhaps a rowboat or motorboat, although it was not moving very fast. It appeared very small at this distance.

The dark-haired mermen swam up not quite to the surface. One of them seemed to grab something below the boat. Finally, Sarah saw. It was a fishing line in the water. The merman grabbed the line and swam downward, yanking a man from the boat into the water. Once under the surface, one of the other mermen threw a net over the man and pulled him down toward the bottom. He screamed, letting out his last breath of air. After a minute or so, another man in the boat stuck his head into the water with a mask on. The third merman was waiting under the boat out of his vision. Once the man's head was in the water, the merman grabbed him stealthily and pulled him into the water. The man tried to fight. He pulled out a knife of some sort, but his hand became tangled in the merman's net. The merman then jabbed him with a trident, and pulled him silently to the bottom.

Sarah wanted to do something to help. She started to swim out to try to rescue the men, but Scallop restrained her. Barracuda and Elwin swam from a nearby rock to help in holding her down.

"You cannot help them now," Elwin whispered in her ear. "And you would give away our position."

"We can take them. They are only three, and we are a dozen," Sarah whispered back.

"There could be more," Barracuda said. "And if one got away, he would report back to the hag, and we would lose the element of surprise. There would be no chance of getting into the hag's lair unnoticed, and our plan would likely fail. It is better not to take the chance. Besides, at this point, there is nothing you can do for them."

Sarah nodded and quit resisting. She looked up and saw that the mermen were now only a hundred yards away. They dumped the bodies of the men. One sank down to the bottom. The other floated slightly, his arms outstretched. She saw the knife fall from his hand, glittering in the dim light. The mermen looked about, as though they had seen some movement in the troop's direction, but finally continued in their patrol, swimming off to the south. Far overhead, the waves had overturned the boat, which now lay capsized. A tackle box and a cooler fell from the boat and sank to the bottom, along with another fishing pole. Soon the boat would also sink, adding to the collection of wrecked vessels.

Once the mermen had gone, they waited until the debris from the boat had settled and then continued their journey across the wreckage-studded plain, moving stealthily as before from rock to ship to coral. It was hard work because of the additional effort required: the constant ducking and crouching, the rapid swimming and stopping, and the overall speed of their movements. It was evident that Barracuda still thought they might run into the enemy.

The expedition continued on for some distance. The planes, boats, and subs seemed to come in groups, as though there were some regions that drew wrecks more than others. Finally, after several hours of swimming, the wrecks were becoming less and less frequent. By this time, Sarah and Lily appeared to be worn out from swimming. Lily in particular was very tired and having trouble keeping up.

"Please, Barracuda, we must rest," Sarah said. "Lily will have trouble making it much farther if we do not stop. Besides, it is a long time after lunch. I can see the sun setting in the west."

"Very well," he said. "I simply wanted to get us clear of the triangle before we stopped again. That was too close a call with the hag's people. They could come back at any time. But it is taking a lot longer than I had expected to get through. Rest here by these rocks for a few minutes and grab a snack, and then we will make one last push to get to a place we can stop and rest unobserved."

The group rested for a few minutes more. When Lily said she had caught her breath, they swam very hard for a longer period of time. Instead of the constant darting and dodging among the obstacles, they swam a little higher and went over the obstacles very quickly. Barracuda would stop every few minutes and look back and up as he waved for them to continue forward. Then, he would sprint to join them. But Lily grew tired and they had to slow at times for her to catch up.

After swimming rapidly on and off for about an hour, they came to a series of rock pillars. These were stacked randomly, some falling over and making arches, some lined up to make long walls, and some standing alone like spires. These formed something of a maze. They entered this maze and dodged left and right through a pathway that only Barracuda seemed to know. It was a little confusing for the girls, but they never feared getting lost because they knew they could swim up and out of the maze at any time. Still, it kept them all out of sight.

After about another quarter hour, they came to a somewhat open area littered by smaller stones. The water here was very warm. A soft red light about a hundred yards ahead brightly lit the area. Finally, they came to a halt.

"We can rest and eat here," Barracuda said.

# 11

## A Brief Rest

The girls immediately plopped down on the ground in the clearing amidst the stones. Once they had caught their breath, they looked around to see where they were. They looked in the direction of the red glow, which was also the source of the heat, and saw about a hundred yards away a small crack in the earth, with a glowing red material coming out of it.

It was magma. They girls had read about this. They could see the water boiling as the magma hit the water and then rapidly cooled, forming a stone pillar that pushed slowly upward. That was the origin of the many stone pillars, Sarah thought. A crack would form as the magma spilled out creating rock until it formed a pillar that covered the crack, and then the magma would find another outlet some feet away. Given the number of pillars, it must have been doing this for hundreds of years.

Many fish and sea creatures seemed drawn to the warmth of the magma. All of the areas near the cracks were teeming with fish and plants. Barracuda and several other mermen approached as close as they could without burning themselves and were able to net a large catch of lobsters, sea cucumbers, flounders, and other fish. They put them on the ends of tridents and pushed them near the magma and then came back again.

As the girls rested, the mermen and Scallop soon laid out a lunch on several of the small boulders on the closer side of the clearing. Once they had cut up the fish, they served them. The girls joined them and took some of the fish. It was warm to the touch. They devoured the fish, which was fully cooked. This was something of a treat for merpeople, as cooked fish was a great delicacy their people did not often enjoy. Normally, the merpeople just ate raw fish. They could not cook without fire, which they could not light underwater, and there was no way to create magma deposits whenever they needed them outside of natural processes. So they always took advantage when they came across such deposits.

After a full and satisfying meal, the girls lay down again to rest, joined by Scallop. She was also visibly tired but was too proud to say anything to Barracuda. Even Elwin, who was a hardened warrior, rested some. With the warmth of the magma after such a strenuous swim, they soon nodded off. When the girls woke up, it was very dim as the sun was setting far overhead. They could see the sun as a distant speck of orange light, but the water was a dark blue overhead, and shadows stretched across the stones and the bottom. Sarah looked around for the others. Were it not for the red light of the magma, they could not have seen each other except as mere shadows. Elwin was gone, as were most of the mermen. Only Sarah, Lily, and Scallop were lying there, and two other shadowy figures stood guard.

When they moved, Barracuda swam up.

"I apologize to you all. I have tried to push you too hard the first day. I forgot that you are not used to deep swimming, and because of the run-in with the hag's soldiers, I was more careful than normal, so it took more time than I expected to get to this point. So I decided to let you rest and use the time to send out spies to look for enemy activity."

"Where is Elwin?" Lily asked Barracuda.

"He went with one group of spies. They will be back soon. The first group that looked north across the triangle has already reported back that they have seen no other movement. Apparently, the patrol we saw was the only one in that area. We will get more reports in shortly."

A few minutes later, another group of mermen swam up from the east, Elwin among them. Sarah and Lily swam out to meet him. He was tired, but otherwise fine and in good spirits.

"Report," Barracuda commanded.

"We swam as far east as the drop off and saw no one," a merman said. "The way is clear in that direction until you get to the very western edge of the Abyss."

"Good," Barracuda said.

"But we will not be able to go that way," the merman continued. "The dark mermen have set up a patrol base at the very edge of the Abyss. Although we saw no one leave from it, we could not pass in this direction. It is as you feared – they are carefully watching the approach from the west."

"Let us wait on the last patrol, for it is in the south that my hopes lie. There, her watch will be relaxed, and we will be able to get to the Abyss unobserved."

"What did you see?" Lily asked Elwin.

"We swam to the edge of the drop off. The ocean floor falls rapidly in a downward slope. It was very dim, so we could not see far, but there was enough light in that location to see the Abyss some distance from where the ocean floor levels out. It was a large crack or cliff, like a canyon out west. There appeared to be large towers on either side. It did not seem impenetrable, for the towers were not that close together."

"These are the watch towers of the merpeople," Barracuda said. "They are not meant as a gate or fence. We built them to keep watch on the hag and her minions. There were eight towers built along the edge of the Abyss, four on each side about a mile apart. From the towers, you can see most of the ground in between. Individuals can probably find a way by hiding among the rocks, but it would be impossible for a great host to pass that way."

"Would it not have been better to build some kind of fence or to have additional towers?" Elwin asked.

"Yes, but this would have required a large army, which the merpeople do not have available," Barracuda answered. "We do not have the strength to contain her completely, only to watch and be prepared to respond if she goes to war. About a year ago, she was able to reclaim the southern towers and now keeps watch on her own borders. While we considered that a loss, it was not devastating to our overall strategy since you can see the lands south of the Abyss for several miles from the towers on the north side. We watch her, and she watches us, but neither of us makes war on the other. Still, it is very troubling that she has expanded her presence at the edge of the Abyss."

"If she occupies the southern towers, how will we get through?" Elwin asked.

"As with the northern towers, individuals may get past," Barracuda answered. "It was my plan to get close enough to allow you three to sneak between the towers, hiding among the rocks. Her gaze will be northward since that is where she will be expecting an attack. We rarely move south of the Abyss because her patrols move that way very often."

It was now completely dark except for the light of the magma. The mermen once again caught and cooked fish in the magma, and Scallop and the girls helped to set the tables, or rather set the boulders. They ate and talked as they waited for the final scouts to come back. Once they finished eating, they set up their tents and sleeping bags - the membranous bags the merpeople provided them - tucked away behind onc of thc pillar walls. The other mermen did the same. With the red glow of the magma, the picnic dinner, and the tents, it reminded Sarah and Lily of the many times they had camped out with their family.

Finally, after about an hour, the last scouts came back. One of the mermen was lying on a rigged stretcher carried by the other two. He appeared to be injured.

"Quick!" Barracuda said, "Get the salve, Scallop!"

Scallop grabbed a bag from among their supplies and swam up to the man. He had two or three puncture wounds, one in his arm and one in his shoulder, with another wound that appeared more as a scratch. All were bleeding profusely. Scallop pulled out a jar of some kind of goo and began to apply it to his wounds. At once, he appeared to recover slightly. The wound on his arm was bleeding the most, but as it was a little more superficial, Scallop was able to stop the bleeding easily. The deepest and most dangerous was the wound in his shoulder, and Scallop wrapped this up in a bandage. She then made him a sling to keep his arm safe.

While Scallop was doctoring the injured merman, the head of the patrol described the encounter. "We went far to the south, as you instructed, turned east, and then came back north in a large arc with the hope of coming within sight of the Abyss and spying out a path to its edge. Alas, we never made it that far. We saw a patrol of half a dozen dark mermen coming from the direction of the Abyss, so we started to retreat only to run into another patrol coming from behind us."

"Where did this patrol come from? Were you not watchful? Did you not have a rear guard as you moved?" Barracuda asked.

"We were as careful as always," the merman replied. "I can say with certainty that we were not followed, and that no other patrols were within sight. There may have been one or two soldiers hidden among seaweed or rocks, but we did not move openly to attract attention, and a patrol of five could not have moved without our seeing them."

"I trust that it is so, for I know you well, Icthus. Where then do you think the patrol came from?" Barracuda asked.

"I know not. It is possible that they were behind us somewhere and have found some means of approaching rapidly and without being seen. Yet their appearance did not seem magical," Icthus said.

"Continue."

"In any case, we were caught in a pincer movement with nearly a dozen dark mermen against us three. We chose to push back against the five behind and fled, but soon a score were following us," Icthus continued.

"A score?" Barracuda asked.

"More mermen must have reinforced them from the Abyss. We continued to fly, stopping only to fend off attacks. It was during one of these encounters that Ray became injured. But we gave out worse than we received. At least one of the dark mermen lies dead, two others were injured, and a half dozen we entangled in nets. It was after this melee that they broke contact when we swam into the far side of the maze of stones. Most of the others had already circled back to the way we came to search for stragglers, and they must have decided they were now too few to pursue us into the maze, so they pulled back. They may not have realized that Ray was injured, as we did not know until we paused and he sank before us," Icthus concluded.

Barracuda asked a few more questions, but then directed them to eat. Scallop and some of the others had kept the food warm for them, and they sat down and ate heartily.

"What now is the plan?" Elwin asked.

"It is clear that we cannot approach from the south, as I had planned," Barracuda said. "Aside from the fact that we have now alerted them to our presence, they appear to be keeping a closer watch on that way than only a few weeks ago. Where all these dark mermen are coming from, I cannot say, other than they must have a base with a lot more men than we might have guessed hidden somewhere out of sight of the towers. Otherwise, our people would have seen them."

"Perhaps they have been sneaking men out a few at a time and have built up a large force that way," Elwin said.

"Perhaps," Barracuda replied. "Or possibly the hag is using her magic to hide them. It is hard to say, but Triton needs to know of this development. Still, it is clear that we cannot go that way."

"But if we cannot approach from the south or to the east, how will we get the humans into the Abyss unseen?" a merman asked. "Go around to the far side of the Abyss and approach in a western direction?"

"That would take many days more than we have to spare," Barracuda said. "I must think on this dilemma. In the meantime, you must get some rest. Set a watch, so the hag's mermen cannot approach."

Everyone except the sentry returned to their tents to lie down for the night. It was a strange feeling that night, sleeping among the waves. They had not previously noticed the gentle lulling of the movement of the water, which made it sort of like sleeping in a hammock. With the dull red glow and the extremely warm water, the girls slept solidly, even after they had taken an earlier nap.

When they awoke the next morning, it was already late in the day. The sun was nearly overhead, and the place was well lit. Sarah and Lily both seemed to wake at the same time and got ready. There was no reason to do so quietly, as the mermen were all outside getting their supplies together, packing everything up, and preparing a final large meal. Ray, the injured merman, sat resting at one of the tables. They ate another fine breakfast of some kind of fish smothered in sea cucumbers. As they ate, several mermen returned from another quick look around, Barracuda among them.

"I let you sleep later today," Barracuda said, "because where we are going will not take a full day. Better that you enter the Abyss after a full night's rest."

"So which will it be?" Elwin asked. "East or south?"

"Neither, actually," Barracuda started to explain. "As I sat and meditated over our situation, it came to my memory that there is another route we could take, a secret route. It would lead us through Atlantis itself and would dump us out at the Abyss."

"Atlantis?" Scallop said. "We dare not go that way."

"Why? Is there some danger?" Sarah asked.

"It is haunted," Scallop said.

"This is the belief of all merpeople," Barracuda said, "including those of the hag, but I have been there before and saw no spirits. I am sure you know the legend. There was a mighty human civilization on the edge of the sea, very advanced for that age. It had alliances and lands stretched throughout the world. However, a volcano destroyed it long ago, and the entire city sank beneath the waves. The merpeople have always considered it a sacred place because it is said that during that age there was an alliance between the merpeople and Atlantis. Unlike men of today, they had frequent contact with fairy peoples, which is where they learned much of what made them great. But we also consider it sacred because it is a graveyard, as we do with the site of the *Titanic* and other tragic shipwrecks. So many died there, it is a place on the edge of the spirit world, which is why so many believe it haunted."

"But I always thought the story of Atlantis was a myth," Lily said.

"I thought it was in the Mediterranean somewhere near Greece," Sarah said.

"It is very real, and it is very close to here. You see, when Atlantis sank, the earth had a different shape, so it is difficult to place within known seas. It is now in a large cavern underneath where we currently swim. There is an entrance not far from here, which is well known to us. But there is also a tunnel on the far side that leads to the Abyss. I came that way accidentally after the battle with the hag, when we were securing the Abyss and building the watch towers. When I let Triton know of it, he ordered us to camouflage it and partially seal it with small stones, but we sealed it loosely. We should be able to push through them.

"This is my plan," Barracuda continued. "We will sneak into Atlantis by the entrance near here under the cover of nightfall. Then we will cross the ruins of the city and come out the next day at the Abyss. From there, Sarah, Lily, and Elwin will descend into the pit, while the rest of us will sneak to the nearest tower to wait for their return. It is really very simple."

"I don't care what you say," Scallop said. "You did not stay there long enough to see the ghosts. I say it is still haunted. Although I have never been there, I have heard the stories of those of our people who have gone to the city and, worse, stayed the night."

"Well, it's either this, or we fight our way past the patrol base so that everyone knows we are here and Sarah and Lily face constant dangers. Or else we give up on the mission entirely and come up with another plan to destroy the Sand Wizard," Barracuda replied harshly.

"We cannot give up," Elwin said. "If this plan is the only one we have to face the Sand Wizard, we must try. He threatens not only the merpeople but all of Fairie."

"Then since it is Sarah and Lily who will face most of the dangers one way or the other, I will leave it up to them which route to take," Barracuda said.

"If we lose all elements of surprise, we will likely be unsuccessful in our quest," Sarah said. "I say we go through Atlantis. Besides, I would like to at least see the great Atlantis so that I know the truth of the stories myself."

Lily agreed, although half-heartedly. Like Scallop, she was a little afraid to go somewhere that has a reputation for being haunted. She never really liked scary movies, preferring instead books and movies with cute, furry animals. Yet even she understood what was at stake. Certainly, she thought, with such a large party they would be safe.

"Good. Then we will leave at suppertime," Barracuda said.

# 12

## Passage through Atlantis

That afternoon, while Scallop, Sarah, and Lily prepared their evening meal, the mermen and Elwin worked to put away all of their things in packs to prepare for the last stage of their journey to the Abyss. The manta rays that had borne their burdens all of this way they prepared to return with two of the mermen, among them Ray, the injured merman.

"I am not sure the manta rays will fit in some of the tunnels leading to Atlantis," Barracuda said. "And since we must send Ray back to Coral with an escort, he can take them. They have served us well. Ray can also take the message of the expansion of the hag's domain and the possible existence of the hidden base. So it will all work out for the best. Of course, that means more of a burden on the rest of us to carry the remaining supplies, but it is only for a short way."

They ate their evening meal early, around mid-afternoon by the position of the sun, and prepared to leave. Ray and the mantas would stay one more night resting before trying to start the long return-journey the next day. Everyone said their goodbyes as they made their last preparations. Then Elwin and the remaining mermen picked up their packs – even Sarah and Lily helped to carry something – and set off to the west, away from the Abyss.

They wove for some minutes through the maze of rock piles at an easy pace. Once they got through the stones and into the open, Barracuda led them to the southwest across a large plain until they reached a large ridge of hills. They crossed these, carefully hiding among the rocks until they reached the top of one hill. They stood for a moment as the sun set in front of them, looking down on the plain on the other side at the edge of the Bermuda Triangle. Sarah could see a downed ship in the distance as they carefully started their descent. By the time they reached the bottom of the hills, darkness had set. Barracuda and another merman at the rear of their file pulled out lanterns with some kind of glowing algae or fungus, which provided a dim light. They could risk no more.

The troop moved from rock to weed as they had before, staying close to the rocky ridge and its protection from prying eyes. They traveled to the south for an hour or so along the ridge until they paused in front of a large outcropping of rock covered with barnacles and coral. It appeared somewhat square-shaped, as though it was man-made, but it was rough around the edges. Rock covered the top, which made it look just like the other rocks on the ridge. Thus, it blended perfectly with the hillside. Only if you looked at it carefully from a close distance would you think it was once a structure of some kind.

"What is this place?" Sarah asked.

"It was once a gate house and tower," Barracuda replied. "There were eight of these gates allowing entrance into the city of Atlantis, according to ancient legend. Rock and stone covered up most of them when they sank, destroying them. This is one of the few that did survive. Those friendly to the city could enter through the gate, which opened by some secret mechanism. After the destruction of the city, the mermen discovered this secret and passed it from one generation to the next, if I can but find it."

Barracuda stopped in front of the stone wall, jutting out at an angle from the cliff, and held his lantern up so he could see the stone. He scanned the outer wall with his hand. He was evidently searching for something.

"There is a mark showing the entrance to the gate house," he said. "Spread out and help me locate it. Without it, it is impossible to find the entrance after all these years."

"What does it look like?" Lily asked.

"It is the symbol for infinity – a sideways figure eight – with a line through it. I do not know what it means in the ancient language of the merpeople or whether it is some sign used by the Atlanteans, but it marks the way to where the entrance is," Barracuda said.

They spread out and searched the rock thoroughly. It did not appear to be on any open surface of the rock.

"Look under the barnacles and coral," Barracuda said. "It should be at around eye level."

The mermen started to break off some of the barnacles. Sarah and Lily looked under the coral growing on the rock until they came to some kind of lichen or plant growing down from a shelf on the outcropping.

"Here it is," Lily said. Sure enough, there was the symbol just as Barracuda described. They went around to the other side of the outcropping, where Barracuda found another symbol. He then went to a large stone among many others about halfway between the symbols where he found a third symbol at foot level.

"We need a lever of some kind or a large stone to press this rock," he said.

"Try this," Elwin said, as he came forward and stepped down on the rock. The rocks started to grind as a trapdoor slowly opened at their feet and a panel on the wall in front of them disappeared into a slot, revealing stairs going down to a tunnel entrance.

"It was evidently made for men," Barracuda said. "Merpeople must use a heavy rock or lever to trigger the opening. Quick! Everyone inside before it closes again. We only have a few seconds."

They all swam down the stairs and into the front of the tunnel. Sure enough, after less than a minute they heard the stones start to grind again until the door shut, sealed without a crack. They were now trapped within the corridor, with only one direction to go. The hallway ran nearly perfectly level and was as smooth as glass, this despite centuries under water. The light from their lanterns reflected off the shiny surface of the rock. It was at least a dozen feet wide, wide enough for a wagon, and about the same distance high, so that even the tallest man could ride a horse or chariot and still not bump his head. They followed Barracuda as he swam through the tunnel, which seemed to go on for at least a hundred yards.

"In the city's heyday, there would have been many positions along the tunnel to protect it against attackers. There would have been unseen gates and a portcullis that they could close, many panels that could open to allow attacks with arrows, and holes above to drip hot oil on anyone who tried to run the gauntlet of the gates," Barracuda said.

They reached the end of the tunnel and came out into an open place. They could see nothing within their vision: no stones or houses or anything to make them think this was an ancient city. There was only a road, which ran as far as they could see in that dim light until it crossed a bridge that ran over a canal. Upward, they could see no roof to the cavern they had entered.

"Although we are but started on this journey, it is now late in the night," Barracuda said. "We do not know what we shall face once we enter the city or how long it will take to cross it. Let us rest here near the tunnel until morning, and then we will proceed through the city."

They all agreed and set up their tents within the tunnel near the opening. Although Lily and Scallop were a little nervous with all the talk about ghosts, they knew the tunnel was safe and that they were in the presence of many men. In the end, they were able to fall asleep, although they all had strange dreams. Scallop dreamed of thousands of people drowning as the city sank beneath the waves. Lily dreamed of spirits rising from their graves in the city – men, women, and children with sad, opaque faces. Sarah dreamed of the city in its glory, with spirits and angels flying in and out as the merpeople swam in and out of their city. She saw the canals in circles, filled with boats and merpeople popping their heads out of the water to talk to the Atlanteans. Others dreamed of the happy people of Atlantis or its fall. Despite the dreams, they all slept solidly.

Sarah was the first to wake the next day. She woke to daylight, which forced her from her reverie as soon as her brain realized that it should not be light since they were in a cave. So she got up out of their tent and went to the end of the corridor and looked out on the city.

"Now that's a sight I will not see again even were I to go to heaven today," she said.

What she saw was this: An immense cavern rose to the height of a stadium before her. The roof of the cavern appeared to be two giant rock projections, several miles long, sticking up out of the cavern floor at ninety degree angles from each other, stretching until they met or crossed at the ceiling of the cavern. In fact, the rock walls held up the cavern like the buttresses of an underground cathedral. The stones met at the top, propping each other up, yet touching only intermittently along a great crack that extended upwards to the top of the ridge under which it existed. This is where the light came from – sunlight from far above filtered down through the crack, illuminating the whole length of the cavern. It was, in fact, rather dim compared to the shallow waters or especially the surface, but compared to the midnight darkness they had seen only hours before, it seemed as bright a day as she remembered. Yet the corners of the cave remained unlit and bathed in shadows, so that she only could see clearly the center of the cavern.

This small glimpse of Atlantis was enough. She could see, stretching from where they camped, seven concentric rings that were canals. These canals were close together on the edge and grew farther and farther apart as they neared the center. Roads came in from every cardinal direction that she could see like a compass rose, each crossing the canals with bridges. Of course, she could only see four, but she guessed that the same pattern was repeated on the other side of the city that she could not see.

Past the first ring, there were the remains of buildings, which grew closer and closer together and taller and taller in height until they reached the center. Some buildings were fallen over, with pillars and columns lying on the ground. Some were buried with debris from the ceilings. Some were in pieces, destroyed by falling rock. In some places, she could see nothing but piles of rubble. And of course on the edges of the city to the left and right, she could see nothing but the large stones stretching to the ceiling, their having destroyed all beneath or above them.

The buildings had something of a Greek look. She saw columns of every style – Ionic, Doric, and Corinthian. She saw images of beautiful human forms in the architecture such as what she had seen at museums. Among them were sphinxlike creatures that reminded her somehow of the Book of Revelation in the Bible. She guessed that these were seraphim or angels. There were also more traditional depictions of angels and fairies, as well as merpeople and other creatures.

At the center of the city was a large hill, with buildings rising up until, at the top of the hill near the ceiling of the cavern, was a large temple or cathedral in almost pristine condition. It seemed very much like a Greek temple, yet there were no carvings of any kind near this temple. Rather, it was plain and unadorned. There were channels for water that once flowed from this temple like a fountain down to the innermost canal. She could see the remains of the watercourse with various spillways, troughs, and pools. She could also see places of open earth where she guessed that trees and bushes once grew, although all vegetation had long rotted, being absorbed by the ocean. In many places, sea plants or coral now grew, enough to give an inkling of what the city might have looked like with trees and other plants.

Above the temple, she could see nothing but a school of colorful fish swimming in the sunlight, like a flock of birds, which reminded her again that it was a place destroyed, a drowned city. Beyond the temple hill, she could see an occasional column or spire that let her know that the city continued on the far side, but she could see nothing else.

Soon, the others woke and came beside her, briefly sharing her vision. Several commented on the beauty of the city. After a moment, however, Barracuda said, "We must be going. Let us eat and then go. We have a mission."

They all snapped to, with some packing up tents and others preparing some food. They ate hastily and then pulled their packs on their backs and started the long swim to the far side. They went quickly down to the bridge, but they slowed as they came near buildings, carefully examining what no other man had seen in a millennia. As they crossed the canals, they saw boat houses, docks where people set sail or sat fishing, and even a few ruined boats overturned here and there. They imagined the commerce that must have taken place here, and possibly the communication with the merpeople along these canals.

After a few minutes, the group crossed into the city proper. They stopped repeatedly to look at buildings. They passed through more than one market, where they saw shops and stands. Were the people here buying and selling when destruction came upon them swiftly? Or were they sleeping soundly in their beds? Sarah wondered, but there was no way of knowing, for there were no indications. They saw the rough huts of the poor on the outer edge of the city, most of which were destroyed except for stone foundations. After a time, they came to wealthier houses with terraces and multiple stories. These were sturdier, and more of them survived the crash, although they were cracked, full of holes, or were missing columns or roofs.

Occasionally, they saw the remains of the citizens, mere skeletons by this time, although there was coral and other organisms attached to the bones, pulling whatever nutrients that were left. Sarah and Lily would often turn their heads as they passed. Although Sarah had read about the remains of Vesuvius and later saw them with her Latin class on a field trip, they were all covered with ash and stone. You could not see the insides, as you could with many of these men. The girls were especially saddened when they saw the small skeletons of children, for they could imagine the terror that came on these little ones.

"It is a tomb," Scallop said. "We are violating the dead. It seems oppressive here to me despite the light. I can feel the ire of their spirits."

"Let's not start imagining things. There is death here, but that does not mean anyone is out to get us. But you are right that we should not dawdle, but move quickly on," Barracuda said.

After an hour or so of navigating the narrow streets zigzagging through the buildings, the troop started the climb up the hill. It was steep, and the road would have been hard, but all they did was swim up until they came to the temple at the top. Around it ran a tall wall of stone enclosing a courtyard. The remains of a rusted iron gate were there, but the gate was mostly gone, leaving a large hole through which they could enter. There, they saw the source of the waterways with a fountain in the center. Just past that was an ancient fire pit, full of watery ash. The doors of the temple were open, with one door hanging from a single hinge. They did not enter because it seemed too holy a place, but they looked in the building and saw an inner curtain, now rotted away. There was a single statue of a man, but it appeared out of place, as though it were a more recent addition. The color of the statue was different from the rest of the stone, and the style seemed incompatible with that of the rest of the building. The statue had been defaced or else a rock fell from the ceiling and struck the head.

"It makes you wonder why the city fell," Sarah commented. "Whether they violated some ancient code or fell away from their God to deserve such a judgment."

"It is obvious that they were blessed indeed," Scallop said, "but perhaps they became jaded by their riches and success, as so many are who do not carefully adhere to the old ways."

Although the temple made them sad, the top of the hill was airy, open, and full of light due to being so much closer to the ceiling. There were not any bodies here, and the destruction was less. Plus, the view was tremendous, so they decided they would stop here and eat their midday meal in the safety of the courtyard. They ate in near silence, perhaps out of some innate sense of stillness or quiet. Once they were through and everyone had had an opportunity to rest, they packed up their things and started swimming down the hill on the far side.

It appeared much the same as the side they ascended; only it was a little narrower. The walls of the cavern came up closer on this side, and there was less of the countryside, less of the canals visible. They could see a road leading away from the hill through houses and markets and over bridges below until it came to a dead end at a stone wall, as smooth as the floor of a hallway. It was just like the wall through which they had passed to enter the chamber, only they had not seen that because it was behind them. They could just make out a tunnel where the road ran. There were towers on either side, but these were crumbling and covered with stone. Above the fifty or so feet of marble wall and towers were rubble and the beginning of the wall of the cavern reaching over their head. This was the only road and tunnel fully visible. They started down the incline toward the small tunnel far away.

They spent the afternoon much like the morning, weaving among buildings and guessing what they had been in that former time. It was much easier as they seemed to float down through the heights, past columns and buildings, until they came to the streets. They continued to swim forward until they were on the road leading out of the city and over bridges. They had not made it to the outer edge of the city when they noticed it was now very dim. It would, in fact, be dark before they made it to the tunnel entrance.

"It is because the light is filtered through the crack," Barracuda said. "Although the sun may be up for another hour up there, it will be dark long before because the sunlight will not be able to make it through the crack. The entire day was shorter because the sunlight filtered in later."

He was right, and although there was a very dim light coming from above, it was not bright enough to see by, and they had to stop and pull out their lanterns just to see the path before them. After another few minutes of swimming, they crossed the bridge over the outer canal and up to the tunnel entrance. All inside was dark and silent.

"Once again, we have reached the end of another day," Barracuda said. "We might swim through the tunnel and reach the entrance to the Abyss by midnight, but it would probably be better to tackle the beginning of your mission alone after you are fully rested. I say we should sleep here for the night near the tunnel and then start the next stage of the journey on the morrow."

They all agreed, and soon they had broken out their tents and fixed dinner. After dinner, they bedded down for the night. They all fell asleep quickly, but at some point during the night, Lily awoke. She looked out of the tent to see if it were morning, and saw something moving across the field before the first canal. It appeared to be a little girl walking. How she could see the girl in the pitch black, she could not say other than the girl appeared to glow slightly. Remembering the trouble she got into when she followed Ishmael without telling anyone, she woke Sarah.

"What is it?" Sarah asked.

"Look!"

Sarah looked out and, seeing the girl, sat upright. "Come on!" she whispered.

They both slipped on their swimming fins, and Sarah grabbed a lantern but kept it covered. They then swam out after the girl. They followed her in silence to the base of the rock that protruded out of the cavern floor. There at the base of the cliff was a pile of rubble that must have once been someone's home. The little girl stopped in front of this and turned to stare at Sarah and Lily. They approached her carefully, but she did not stir.

"Who are you?" Sarah finally asked.

"My name I cannot remember," she said, "for it has been ages upon ages since I have seen another human form. I once lived here, in a house which stood right there." She pointed at the rubble.

"What happened?" Lily asked.

"When the earthquake started, I had only a few seconds to respond. I had a necklace given to me by the fairy peoples to protect me. I used it to prevent rock from falling on me and the water from drowning me, yet I was trapped. I could not escape, and there was no one to rescue me. I lived on for some days, but eventually I died."

"You mean ... in there?" Lily asked.

"Yes. I have been waiting for ages for some purpose. This is why my soul has not been released. Your coming must be the reason why I have tarried. It must be some purpose of the fairies or the angels. You must find my necklace. Then I will find eternal peace."

The girls turned to the rubble and started to dig. It was hard work, and took several minutes to clear out the stones one by one. Finally, they came upon a large recess beneath the rock. It was shaped like a dome, and the stones were now fitted and sealed together like a ceiling. Sarah knocked a hole in it, and water started to pour inside. It had been protected for ages against the ravages of the ocean. Sarah held her lantern up and peered inside. Something glittered. They saw inside the silver necklace of the poor girl in almost pristine condition on top of an aquamarine robe, neatly folded. Where the little girl was, she could not say, other than she must have been released to go to heaven. Sarah picked the necklace up. It was a silver chain with a medallion with the same symbol she had seen at the gate to Atlantis – an infinity symbol with a line through it. Sarah slipped the necklace around her own neck. They then took the stones and covered the hole and whatever remained within completely, like a grave.

When they turned to thank the girl, she was gone. She was at peace. Sarah and Lily returned to the camp and got back into their tent. In a few minutes, they were asleep again.

# 13

## Into the Abyss

The next day, the expedition woke up as soon as the sun was shining down from the ceiling of Atlantis, which meant that it was at least mid-morning. They packed up their tents and ate a leisurely breakfast. After everyone had finished, they pulled on their packs, took out their lanterns, and started down the tunnel.

Unlike the tunnel through which they entered, this tunnel seemed severely damaged. Although it ran smooth for some dozen yards, the troop soon ran into numerous cracks. A little farther, there were piles of rubble on the floor, and then a cave-in on the right side of the tunnel narrowed it to only a few feet wide. Once they passed the cave-in, they came to an opening in the ceiling, and several feet of debris covered the entire floor of the tunnel. Barracuda swam up, looked around, and then returned.

"Looks like it was a guard room over the tunnel," he reported. "There are still arms racks with cross-bows hanging on the wall. There is a fireplace and some cooking implements. I think they kept guard by watching those below them, but of course the floor over the tunnel is gone."

They continued to swim down the tunnel, which exited past the collapsed room above them. Onward they swam for another score of yards through the tunnel, cracked and full of debris. Finally, they came to a dead end, where the tunnel was full, not of large debris, but small stones and pebbles. The pile of stones completely blocked off the end of the tunnel.

"This is the spot I spoke of before," Barracuda said. "The merpeople piled up these stones to seal off the tunnel and hide it from those coming from the Abyss, which is just on the other side. We must dig out the stones to get through."

The group formed a line and started to clear out the stones one at a time, passing them down the line and placing them behind them. The mermen did most of the heavy lifting, with the help of Elwin, but the girls helped move some of the smaller stones or would organize the pile of stones behind them to keep them from blocking the tunnel in case they had to return the way they came. They worked from the top to the bottom until there was a small sliver of light coming through the top of the stones.

After a few more minutes of digging, Barracuda said, "We need to extinguish all of the lamps. It is light out, but it is still dim in the Abyss, and someone might notice the lantern light coming through."

They did as he said, placing their group in pitch darkness other than the sliver of dark blue light coming over the top of the stones. The mermen raked the stones over quickly to enlarge the hole and provide additional light. They continued to clear the stones away until there was a large-enough opening over the top to allow them to swim through one at a time. Barracuda went through first, followed by one or two of the other mermen. Last came Sarah, Lily, and Elwin.

On the other side of the stones, the mermen were still in the tunnel, which extended another yard or two, but it was rougher on this side as though it had been severely damaged. The mermen hid on the edges of the tunnel and were looking up. A dim blue light streamed down from above, revealing a few feet of the tunnel opening. It was midday far above them. They could look up and see the shallower water and sunlight, but at their level it was darker, and below them, the light faded into darkness.

Out of the opening of the tunnel, they could see the Abyss. It was a giant canyon or crack in the ocean floor. They could see it extending for some distance in front of them until it disappeared around a curve. It was about two or three hundred feet wide directly above them, but farther away it seemed like it was a good quarter to half-mile across. The bottom of the canyon dropped below them into the darkness, going on for some unknown distance, which, according to what Barracuda had told them, went on several miles. The tunnel itself was about fifty to a hundred feet below the ocean floor inside the Abyss itself, which lay half in shadow.

Ahead and above the group was the first of the towers Barracuda had described. It went straight up from the edge of the Abyss. The walls of the tower were smooth, without stone or mortar visible, rising about fifty feet, and at the top was a rounded dome roof. They could see no doors or openings at the base on this side of the tower. They could just make out a light coming from a window at the top of the tower. On the other side of the Abyss a little to their right, they could see the twin of the tower. They were identical in size and shape, and the girls could see a light in the other tower as well. Sarah knew that some of the enemy mermen were at the top, watching for Triton's people. Some ways ahead, they saw another tower, and then another, extending off into the distance.

Sarah had half expected the Abyss to be a dead and empty place, but it was not so. The drop was steep, but there were many shelves and caves along the edge, and in some places the drop was more gradual. As they looked out, they could see buildings and paths or roads on some of the shelves, the closest about two hundred yards away. Some had lights in the window, and far away, they could see a merman swimming between buildings. These shelves and buildings extended far into the darkness. They could see the twinkling of lights far below them.

Barracuda held his hand up to his lips to quiet them. Then he whispered to the other mermen, "Try as best as you can to pile the stones back up so as to hide any trace of the tunnel."

The mermen silently complied.

"Our plan has changed somewhat," Barracuda said quietly. "I had planned on taking you to one of the towers, where you could study maps of the Abyss and learn where you need to go. We could have given you supplies and let you rest before beginning your journey into the dark. Because of the expansion of the hag's watchfulness and our flight through Atlantis, this is no longer possible. We will have to give you what aid we can now. First, we will rearrange the packs so that you will have enough supplies to last you several days. We can get to the towers and resupply there. Of course, you will have to carry the packs, if you think you are up to that."

"I think I can," Lily said, who was not only shorter than her sister but slighter in build.

"If we don't have a map, how will we know the way?" Sarah asked.

"It might take a little more time to explore, but I will give you what directions I can to at least provide you with guideposts. The hag's grotto is at the back of a long narrow tunnel. I understand that her slaves have been mining it for some years, so there is no clear map of the way. But I can say that if you follow the older, natural tunnels and not the more recently excavated mine shafts, you should find the way. As for the entrance to her tunnel, it is about a mile down and guarded by two towers built onto a shelf in the Abyss," Barracuda said.

"The only other advice I can give you is to stay hidden as much as possible," he added. "Your weapon is stealth. You must avoid detection. Avoid her guards and even her slaves as much as you can. When you get into her lair, if you can get Triton's trident without confronting Hagatha, do so. Although she may appear old, she is very dangerous, especially her voice. And her potions. Do not under any condition eat of the food she offers you.

"Now you must go. We will wait until you are ready and then swim to the tower to distract anyone watching. Do not look at us, but swim down and out of sight. If you return ... when you return ... meet us at this first tower. We will be waiting for you," he concluded.

Sarah and Lily got their packs and hugged Scallop. Elwin grasped the forearm of Barracuda as a sign of fidelity, as was the custom of the mermen. They then swam silently off the ledge and into the darkness as Barracuda, Scallop, and the rest of the mermen started swimming in small groups along the north wall of the Abyss toward the nearest tower. For a moment, the girls paused to watch them swim across the Abyss toward the tower. Shortly after, the first of the mermen disappeared behind it.

At about the same moment, Sarah, Lily, and Elwin heard a gong ring out under the water, an alarm perhaps from the tower on the opposite side of the Abyss, where they had seen lights like eyes watching from the tower. The watchers must have seen the mermen swimming around the tower. Suddenly, Sarah and Elwin felt extremely vulnerable. They started to swim down, but Lily sat entranced looking up at the tower. Something drew her attention there, some evil or power at work. No one spoke, but Elwin pulled at her elbow repeatedly until some seconds later, she finally snapped out of her trance and started to move.

Sarah, Lily, and Elwin swam straight down into the Abyss as hard as they could, not bothering to stop to see if anyone was leaving the tower or following them. They kept to the shadows and the side of the pit to avoid being seen as much as possible. After a moment, they stopped under a ledge to catch their breath.

"Do you think they spotted us?" Sarah whispered.

Elwin looked up, but could see no one moving against the light of the sky above them. No one was moving from the tower, which he could easily see in the slanting afternoon sun, and no one was coming around it into the Abyss. "I don't see anyone," he whispered back. "But that does not mean that they have not notified others. There are many caves and outbuildings where their soldiers might hide. We had better keep moving."

The three of them rested a minute more, and then continued down into the pit of the Abyss, a little slower but still with purpose. As they swam down, it became darker and colder. The temperature dropped suddenly, making them glad of the wet suits the elves had given them. The world of light, already distant, faded from view until it was nothing more than a mere crack of deep blue far overhead. Around them, it was not midnight black. There were too many lights for that. There were twinkling lights in windows of buildings or coming out of caves. Every now and then, a door or shutter would open, allowing more light to flood the canyon walls from some point.

At first, the buildings were mostly on the southern side of the Abyss, but after the towers were far out of view, they were on both sides. It was in fact a city of merpeople, but was distributed vertically along the pit rather than horizontally in the sun. It was hard to estimate the size because the houses were set vertically and spaced out on the ledges, but Sarah guessed that the entire city was about a quarter of the size of Coral. It probably contained only a few hundred merpeople compared to the thousands in the city of King Triton.

The buildings were of various shapes and sizes. Some were mere shacks of driftwood. Some were of stone. Some sat alone on the ledges, some extended out from the walls. Some were mere doors blocking off the entrance to a cave. The caves seemed to have various entrances, like an ant farm. The roads were all short, going from one cave to another, as though it were not safe to be out for long. The girls saw no public market and no trading, but they heard wheels turning in some factory. They did see what they could only describe as blacksmiths inside shops hammering on metal, so there were evidently industries of some kind in the Abyss.

The three of them could see merpeople moving back and forth in the shadows from one building to another, all busy with unknown tasks. The ones they could see in the light were similar to the mermen they had seen in the Bermuda Triangle – pale skin and dark hair. Lily suddenly understood their appearance, for here were a people who rarely saw the sun, who never tanned and never had their hair bleached. Whatever the tasks were that took up their time, they all seemed related to battle. The dark mermen were a warlike people. Most carried weapons of some sort, and the only industries they saw were related to making weapons and armor.

Sarah, Lily, and Elwin continued to keep to the shadows and prayed that they would not run into anyone. Since most of the dwellings seemed to be on the south side of the Abyss, they stayed mostly on the north side, and they avoided the largest concentration of buildings by remaining on the outskirts to the west or east of these settlements. Nevertheless, all three knew they risked discovery as long as they were in the area, for they occasionally saw mermen traveling close to them on some unknown errand. It was amazing to Sarah that they could have gone so far without being seen and an alarm raised, but in truth far too few of the mermen left their homes or caves for more than a few feet. The place seemed to smell of fear, though whether it was fear of the dark, fear of some unknown creatures that swam up from the deep, or fear of their chieftains and the hag she could not say. In any case, even with the few lights, it was very dark, and the girls found that they could hide in the shadows and continue on their way into the depths unseen.

Occasionally, as they swam, the trio also saw mysterious creatures of the deep, though it was rare when they did. They did see some schools of fish, strange white fish with large bulbous eyes. The fish were clearly blind and crossed one another in random patterns. They saw one or two other creatures, mostly strange fish with large teeth and jaws, and once they saw an octopus or squid of large size, but it moved past them quickly out of the Abyss and into the ocean depths. Despite this wealth of ocean life, the three never saw any of the dark mermen fishing, at least not there in the Abyss. Sarah could only guess that the food produced in those depths was evil-tasting or even poisonous.

After nearly an hour of swimming, Sarah, Lily, and Elwin came to what they thought were the outskirts of the merman city in the Abyss. Buildings and lights were fewer and farther between. They stopped to rest again inside a small recess on a ledge on the north side of the canyon that hid them from sight. There below them some hundred yards on the opposite side from their ledge, they saw the twin towers described by Barracuda. The towers were not as large as the watch towers they had seen on the edge of the Abyss. Rather, they were only twenty or so feet tall, but they had the same domed roof and the same watchful lights as the others they had seen. Between the towers was a raised gate of corroded metal. Behind the gate they saw a dark tunnel like a maw between two sets of eyes.

"We're going in there?" Lily asked in wonder.

"How will we get through the gate and past the eyes?" Sarah considered.

"Well, it appears that the windows look out into the Abyss, as though they are looking more for people approaching from a distance. I do not see any windows looking inward. I think if we could sneak up to the base of the towers, we could probably make a rush into the cave. The real question is how will we get close to the towers without being seen?" Elwin said.

"Maybe the gifts of the Elf King," Lily said.

"That is right!" Sarah said. "I have the cloak. But what good will that do us? It will only get one of us up to the tower."

"Not if we share," Elwin said.

Thus, the three of them devised a plan for Sarah to move each of them close to the tower under the cloak, one at a time, starting with Elwin. Then she would return for Lily. Once they had assembled, they would make a rush between the towers and into the cave.

It was difficult work. Although too large even for Sarah, the cloak was not meant for two, and they had to move carefully to keep both Sarah and Elwin covered up, making adjustments every few feet to cover a leg here or an arm there. It was also difficult to navigate. They could not properly swim with a cloak on – when Sarah tried, she almost kicked the cloak off of her. Without being able to keep up momentum, they sank rapidly. Plus, it was hard to see with the cloak on to aim for the tower. In the end, they landed some dozen yards below the towers.

Sarah encountered the same problem swimming back for Lily, who remained hidden on the ledge. Sarah landed lower than she meant to and had to swim up some ways to get to the ledge. The way back with Lily was a little easier, for she was smaller, and there was more room in the cloak. Yet she was also in a greater hurry, in part because it had taken so much time to go across with Elwin that she started to get nervous that the watch would increase. On one occasion, she kicked the cloak off both of them, but she recovered in seconds. From the tower, they would have seen only a flicker of a person, certainly not enough time for watchers to see, let alone respond.

Finally, Sarah, Lily, and Elwin were all together beneath the towers. Once again using the cloak, they moved one at a time until they were at the base of the left-hand tower. Elwin took the cloak and then moved in front of the gate to spy out the situation before returning.

"As I suspected, there is not a sentry on this side of the gate. There might be one or two guards on the other side of the gate. I could not see that far, but we could move past them quickly. The towers are there to watch for and protect against a large invasion force or sea creatures that use no other stealth than the darkness. There is an open gate, but we can get beyond it before anyone would notice and lower the portcullis. There are also holes for crossbows, but the chance that anyone is watching at this point is low. I suggest that we swim hard through the gate and deal with what is on the other side if it becomes necessary. They may sound an alarm, but we would be inside and could hide," he said.

They all agreed. Sarah put on the cloak again and swam out to take one last look. With the coast clear, she signaled to the others, and they swam rapidly around the corner and through the center of the two towers. A light was shining through holes in the two side walls at about shoulder level. Following Elwin, the girls swam under the holes and beneath the beams of light. They passed the portcullis and came to a large chamber with several tunnels leading out the other side. Two dark mermen lay between them and one of the tunnels. Two other tunnels were to their right and somewhat behind them.

The girls paused briefly, but the two sentries appeared focused on the tunnel. They were evidently guarding people exiting the tunnel, not entering it. Suddenly, the guards started to turn to the center tunnel, which was clearly in the field of vision of the other two tunnels. They were sentries and were moving from tunnel to tunnel. Without thinking, Elwin and Sarah headed straight toward the nearest tunnel as fast as they could go. They only had a few seconds to make it before the mermen turned to face them. They kicked extra hard and sped into the tunnel. They swam down the tunnel a ways, but Lily seemed to be pausing, looking back at where they came.

"Lily, hurry up. Do you want them to see you?" Sarah whispered.

"But this is one of the new tunnels," Lily said. "Barracuda said we are to go down the old natural tunnel. We are going the wrong way!"

# 14

# The Undersea Mines

Sarah and Elwin both realized that Lily was right and that they had headed down one of the new mine shafts. According to Barracuda, the new mine shafts led away from the older, natural tunnel that led to the hag's grotto.

"It can't be helped now," Elwin said. "We must continue moving before the guards see us."

They swam some way down the tunnel and then stopped to see if they were being followed. All they heard was silence other than their breath escaping as bubbles. The tunnel was very dark at that point, and they saw no lights coming from behind them. After a few minutes frozen there listening, Elwin finally breathed easier.

"It looks like they did not see us. We are pretty far down the tunnel. I think we can risk a light now, so we can see where we are going."

Elwin pulled out a lantern and uncovered the glowing algae inside. He and the girls were in a fairly round shaft, but it was obvious the tunnel had been recently excavated. They could see the pick marks on the stone, and someone had dug up and carted away the rock on the floor.

The three of them swam down the tunnel, twisting and turning until they came to the first of several intersections, with rough tunnels leading off randomly in different directions. All of the tunnels were relatively new and recently dug out by the use of tools. They were all roughly the same size and diameter. There was little to distinguish one tunnel from another other than perhaps an unusual rock or the way the tunnel turned. They all realized that they would get hopelessly lost in minutes if they continued along the tunnels.

The girls paused for a moment, wondering which way they should go. Elwin started to just pick one of the tunnels and scratch a mark on the wall to remember which way they had tried.

"Wait," Sarah said. She suddenly remembered reading the myth of Theseus and the Minotaur in the Labyrinth. For a girl her age, she was very well read. She took her shirt, which she had quit wearing days ago, and started to unravel the material until she had a long piece of thread. She continued to unravel it until she had many dozens of yards of string. Elwin understood at once, but Lily did not see until Sarah tied the end of the thread to a rock and started to unwind it as they swam down the tunnel. They now no longer had to worry about getting lost, at least until they ran out of thread.

"But what about the mermen?" Lily asked. "Will they not follow the string to find us?"

"Perhaps," Elwin responded. "But it is dark in here, so they may not see it. Even if they see it, they may not know what it is. You must remember that the merpeople know nothing of our weaving process or have ever heard of cotton."

The trio started down the tunnel again, Sarah unwinding as they went. They continued for some time, turning this way and that, exploring every avenue, knowing that they could always retrace their steps. In fact, they had to do so repeatedly, for they often went the wrong way and came to dead ends, to what were obviously mining shafts shored up with braces of wood or bone, and to obstacles such as large holes. They would then backtrack, rewinding the string as they went, until they came back to where they could try a different route.

The girls and Elwin went carefully and quietly, afraid that they would run into guards or other people who would raise an alarm that they were there. As Barracuda had observed, they had to rely on stealth, and being discovered would end their efforts to steal Triton's trident back, even if they could escape. They stopped only occasionally to eat or rest, and then only briefly in an out-of-the-way corner and always with someone watching for mermen coming up the tunnels.

At first, the three of them did not see anyone. They seemed to be in an area of old mine shafts, long abandoned. There was no evidence of recent digging, and they often ran into piles of debris blocking the tunnels, where the shoring had collapsed and the mines caved in. At one such cave in, they found a skeleton trapped beneath a pile of rubble. The person had died where he had fallen, though whether the rock crushed him, he had suffocated, or others left him to starve they could not tell. The girls and Elwin took their first rest not more than a dozen yards from the remains, and even through Elwin doused the lights, it took a long time for Sarah and Lily to fall asleep knowing the skeleton was there. They eventually got a few hours of sleep, but not enough for them to feel completely rested.

Eventually, as the three of them backtracked, they came to more recent excavations. It was at this point that they came across what they had been dreading – other people in the mineshafts. The girls and Elwin entered a large and open cavern where new digging was starting. They could see across the cavern a group of mermen. They quickly doused their lantern. Most of the mermen were obviously from Coral or at least from the surface. They could see the blond hair and bright colors of the mermen who were working in the shafts. They were moving in and out of the tunnels carrying buckets of rock, which another group was examining and sorting. Above them were several dark mermen holding tridents, watching the surface mermen and occasionally prodding them when they moved too slowly.

The girls sat watching silently as Sarah pulled up her string so that no one would follow it. Elwin motioned for them to follow him. They crept silently across the cavern to another tunnel opposite them, swimming as low to the ground as possible. The other mermen were far away on the other end of the cavern and did not see them cross. The three got into the other tunnel and went some ways down before Elwin risked pulling out the lantern again.

Sarah, Lily, and Elwin continued along the tunnel, but much more slowly and carefully now. Sensing they might run into another mining party at any time, they turned corners only after looking first and kept the lantern covered other than a beam showing on the floor. They said nothing, but moved silently through the tunnel. After a few minutes, they stopped to rest. After they caught their breath, they heard what sounded like sobbing.

"Do you hear that?" Sarah whispered.

"It sounds like someone crying," Lily said.

"Where is it coming from?" Elwin asked.

They turned a corner and noticed that there was a narrow crack on one side of the tunnel. It was, in fact, the entrance to a small branch of a tunnel that led to a small cave or room. Elwin shined the light of the lantern around the room. There in one corner was a mermaid, her hands covering her face, weeping. When the light fell on her, she immediately arose.

"Please do not hurt me. I was on the way to get the food and got lost," she said.

"What are you doing here?" Sarah asked.

"Who are you?" the mermaid asked. "You are not one of the hag's mermen. You are not mermen at all but humans. And an elf," she added as Elwin opened up the lantern to allow more light into the room. "How is it that you are underwater and breathing?"

"We are here on a secret mission. The merpeople sent us and are helping us," Elwin said. "What is your name?"

"My name is Shelly. You are here to rescue us?" she asked.

"Well, Shelly," Sarah started. They had not really talked about the captive merpeople or what the plans were for them. Yet she knew if they could get the trident, the merpeople would be released from her spell and could do what they wanted. "If we are successful, you will be able to escape."

"Please take me with you. You must take me when you leave. Do not leave me here," Shelly said.

Sensing a trap, Elwin asked, "How is it that you are able to talk to us if you are under enchantment to work in the mines?"

"The hag has decreed that we are to work in the mines, carry food, or whatever our task, and that we will not leave. Yet she does not control our every action. That would require her constant presence, and she is too lazy. Instead, she uses her guards to manage day-to-day activities. That allows us some freedom, although her magic compels us not to leave, and we are more compliant in doing the tasks they give us. Yet she never dictated that we could not talk or yearn for freedom," Shelly said.

"So then you are not a mindless body of slaves as the merpeople suspected?" Elwin asked.

"No. We are quite aware of our surroundings, only we cannot gain release from them. Please. Promise me you will come back for me, that you will set our people free," Shelly said.

"Of course we will come get you," Lily said.

"Lily, we cannot make such a promise. We do not know if we will be successful or how we will get away," Sarah admonished.

"Wait," Elwin said. "If we can release the merpeople and they are not brainwashed, we can use their help to escape. Sarah is right, of course, that we cannot make a promise. But I can promise we will do all that we can to set you free, and if we are successful, we will lead you out. Take heart."

Shelly looked at them and smiled. "I had better get back to work before someone misses me. I will get ready. There are several others ..."

"That would be bad. If she tells others, the guards may overhear or they may be ordered to betray us," Sarah said. "That would ruin any chance of surprise."

"I don't know. Maybe we are being too careful," Elwin said. "It is unlikely that the hag will directly command them to talk unless a guard tells her. On the other hand, if she can tell a few key leaders to be prepared to fight when the spell ends, we would have a lot soldiers to fight the dark mermen. Perhaps it would be good for her to spread the news, but she would need to do it discreetly, without the guards learning of our plans. Do you think you can accomplish this, Shelly?"

"We share many secrets that the guards do not know. I can let our people know without tipping off the dark mermen," she replied.

"Then go quietly and quickly. Do not raise suspicions, and we will come for you," Elwin said.

Sarah and Lily hugged Shelly and then grasped her forearm in a sign of promise. "I will do as you ask," the mermaid said. Then she left the cave and swam off down the tunnel back toward the cavern.

Elwin and the girls waited for a few minutes to make sure she was safely away. Then they crept out of the cave and returned to their flight along the tunnel.

The trio continued for some way as they had before, unwinding the string and then rewinding it as they retraced their steps. They found a crack that led to another cave above one of the mine shafts. It appeared to be a natural cave and never used, so Elwin risked their resting once again. They crept into the cave and covered their lantern, taking turns on watch as they slept. After they had gotten sufficient rest, they continued on down the tunnel.

Finally, after several more hours of exploring and searching, they came to a large natural tunnel. At first, they thought it was a mine shaft because it had also been improved – rocks removed, openings enlarged, and stalactites and stalagmites removed. Yet after a few feet of going down the tunnel, they realized it was a series of natural caverns and tunnels and not an excavation. Unlike the mineshafts, there were too many odd turns and holes, the spacing was uneven, and the floor was sandy instead of rock. It was easy to compare because there were numerous side tunnels carved into the rock. They had located the natural tunnel leading to the hag's grotto.

"This is it," Elwin said. "This is the main path to the hag's headquarters. Now we must be more careful than ever. We will have to keep the lights dim and be more watchful for others. I imagine her guards come this way frequently."

It took only a few minutes for Elwin to be proven correct. The girls saw a light coming from ahead, so they quickly doused their light and hid down a side tunnel. A dark merman swam rapidly by alone, obviously a runner of some sort because he carried no weapons. A few minutes later, he returned, and they hid again. Then after about an hour, they heard the sound of numerous creatures behind them swimming. It was a host of mermen coming up the tunnel. The girls thought the hag's mermen must have discovered them or found out their plans!

"Where can we go?" Sarah asked.

Elwin looked around until he saw a small ledge high up close to the ceiling of the cavern they had just entered. It could hold all of them and was out of the field of vision of people traveling along the tunnel. "There!" he cried.

Sarah, Lily, and Elwin swam up and tucked themselves away on the shelf, quickly dousing their light again once they had made it to the top. No sooner than they had hid, a light came around the corner. One of the captains of the dark mermen was floating watching with an aide while four or five lines of mermen swimming in formation entered the cavern and then went toward a side tunnel the girls had not seen. It took several minutes for the host to swim by. There must have been at least a hundred of the dark mermen.

The captain continued to watch as they swam past. Suddenly, the same runner swam up from the main tunnel ahead.

"Queen Hagatha bids you go at once around the Abyss and attack Triton's towers. If you come from the rear, you will surprise them."

"I wonder why the queen suddenly wants us to attack," the captain said. "We have been maintaining a delicate balance with the merpeople for so many years. We are not yet at our full strength. We are still dealing with the sea elves to the north, and we have yet to gather the Kracken and other sea creatures to us as our allies."

"She now has formed a stronger alliance," the runner said. "You know that through her magic she talks to the Sand Wizard. It is through his counsel that she is now making her move."

"I have doubts of this Sand Wizard. He is not of the merpeople," the captain complained.

"Do you doubt the queen?" the runner replied. "She would be displeased to hear of it."

"You little squealer," the captain replied. "I said no such thing. I am following orders, as you can see, and I remain loyal to the queen. But I have spoken openly that I doubt the reliability of the Sand Wizard. Who is to say he will help and reward us if we help him? He cannot be trusted. I can only trust that the queen has thought this through, as I have often bid her. But you can tell her from me that her command is my desire. I will follow her instructions to the letter."

The runner swam off down the tunnel, and the captain turned to follow the host down the other tunnel. The girls and Elwin waited a few minutes. When they saw the coast was clear, they came down from the shelf.

"Well, the war has started," Elwin said. "Together, the hag and the wizard are making their move on the merpeople."

"I wish we could warn King Triton or the elves or someone," Lily said.

"They will be watching," Sarah said. "Barracuda will not be surprised."

"I hope that you are correct," Elwin said. "Now how is it that the mermen are able to get out without leaving the Abyss?"

Elwin swam over to the tunnel where the host had gone. He examined it closely.

"Look at this tunnel. See how it slopes gently up toward the surface? It must be another way out. That is how they have been able to sneak out without being seen. That is how they snuck up on Barracuda's scouts when they approached from the south. It is not a fortress, but a highway from the realm of Hagatha to the surface. It would come out many miles from the Abyss itself. That is how they plan on attacking. Sneaking out the back way unseen and then going around for miles.

"Come, we must hurry," Elwin concluded.

Elwin, Sarah, and Lily swam rapidly down the tunnel toward the hag's grotto, not caring whether they were seen. They knew they were close to the end, and it was time for the confrontation.

# 15

# The Sea Hag's Grotto

The girls and Elwin swam down the tunnel not knowing exactly what to expect. Soon, the passage widened into an enormous open space. It seemed, momentarily, as though they had left the caves and were now somewhere near the surface. Above them, a light shone brightly like the sun, and the water was warm, not cold like in the mine shafts. Stretching in front of them was a forest of undersea plants – coral, seaweeds, and kelps of all varieties – along with all of the undersea creatures of the shallow waters. There were anemones, urchins, jellyfish, and schools of various tropical fish. They could see paths cutting through the forest bound by rocks and coral, making it more like a garden or park. Far away, they could see a rock shelf with a series of openings into caves – the grotto home of the sea hag.

At first, Lily thought that perhaps they had been going gradually up toward the surface and that they were now back on the continental shelf. But then she saw the walls of the cavern they were in arching far above them. Somehow, the enormous cave was full of light. A mass of glowing algae, similar to their lanterns but far larger and brighter, was at the top of the cavern, beaming down like the sun. The heat, they guessed, came from some volcanic cracks in the cave, similar to the ones they had seen near the surface. Hagatha must have transported the plants from the surface to make a home away from home and then sculpted them into a garden where she could swim for leisure or take tours with her escorts. Sarah remembered reading about the Seven Wonders of the World, including the Hanging Gardens of Babylon. This undersea garden should certainly be listed among them, if only anyone knew about it, Sarah thought.

"That must be the hag's lair," Elwin said, pointing to the caves on the far side of the cavern. "We should head that way."

They started swimming toward the caves, when they saw a dark merman leave one, swimming straight toward the tunnel from which they came.

"Quick! Hide!" Sarah said.

They all swam down into a bed of seaweed. They watched the merman swim far above them, giving no thought to the garden below him. The garden was, they realized, the perfect cover and the only way they could approach the hag's grotto unseen.

After the merman passed, they swam just slightly above the weeds, sometimes darting into some kelp or behind a coral formation to hide from passers-by. Sometimes they would go down one of the paths when the vegetation became too thick or to avoid a jellyfish or other sea creatures. Yet they moved steadily across the cavern jungle until they came to the base of the rock wall leading up to the cave where Hagatha made her palace.

Just as they were about to swim up to scout out the area and develop a plan, they heard a commotion behind them, so they remained hidden among the weeds at the base of the cliff. Coming toward them was a chain of a dozen merpeople of various colors – obviously surface merpeople – tied together by a long rope and escorted by half a dozen dark mermen. The guards guided the line of merpeople into the cave entrance on the cliff and out of sight above them.

Elwin and the girls looked behind them to see if anyone else were coming, and, seeing no one, crept up the cavern wall and peered into the entrance. Inside, they saw a spacious cave set out like the great hall of a keep, except that instead of columns there were stalactites and stalagmites and other rock formations from a previous age and instead of a dais and throne was a mound of stone and debris with a chair sculpted from some of the same material. In addition to stone, there were bones, moss, and driftwood. The seat of the throne was a piece of driftwood tied down by dead vines; the back was the rib cage of some fish; and the padding was moss. Topping the throne was the skull of a large fish or whale. The palace space included both a receiving room and private quarters. They could see through the openings between the cave's columns and rock formations a dim bedroom and dining area in separate rooms of her grotto. There was a bedroom with several large mirrors hanging on the wall, a dining room with a table set out, and even a lounge or den of some sort. But the light and focus of the action was on the throne.

The guards escorted the merpeople until they were in front of the throne. On the throne sat an older but still very beautiful mermaid. She had raven hair with streaks of gray at the temples with a purple tail tucked around the side of the throne.

"And what do we have here?" she asked.

"Surface merpeople," a guard said, "found wandering in our domains in the Bermuda Triangle. We captured them and brought them here to serve you."

"Ah, another group to work in the mines," she said vindictively. She reached next to the throne and picked up a trident lying next to the throne. Holding it in front of her, she said, "I command you to work in the mines for the remaindcr of your days, to never try to escape, and to obey the commands of the guards set over you."

As she spoke, the trident started glowing. The merpeople hung their heads, and the guards started to lead them away. She then placed the trident next to her throne again.

"It's Triton's trident," Elwin whispered, pointing.

Sarah, Lily, and Elwin ducked down and then hid among the plants growing at the base of the cliff. The guards led the merpeople out while Elwin and the girls sat and talked.

"Did you see the size of that one mirror?" Sarah asked. "And that weird throne?"

"Yes, she really is vain," said Lily.

"I think I have an idea," Elwin said. "Who is the fastest swimmer?"

"Probably Sarah," Lily said. "She is bigger."

"What we need is a distraction so someone can get the trident, which is the object of our being here. While two of us distract her, the other could swim in quickly, grab the trident, and then get away," Elwin said.

"What kind of distraction?" Lily asked.

"Well, we could try to attack her somehow," he replied. "It would have to be something to draw her away from her throne."

"I don't know," Sarah said. "That seems dangerous. She is a hag and could use her magic on us if she gets angry. Not to mention she would call all of her guards."

"The hag's magic consists mainly of her voice and her potions, according to the Sea Elf King," Elwin said. "As long as we don't eat or drink anything and don't listen to her, we should be safe enough."

"Why don't we just get captured and brought before her," Lily said. "That way she would only be talking to us, and we could escape after Sarah gets the trident. It would be easy. See, there are more guards swimming overhead even now."

They looked up, and she was correct. Another group of dark mermen swam into the cavern leading another mermaid.

"Isn't that the mermaid we saw in the mines?" Elwin asked.

"Yes," Sarah and Lily said together. "It is Shelly."

"They must have found her hiding," Sarah added.

"I think Lily's plan is the best we have at this point. And it will give us a chance to free the mermaid," Elwin said, as the guards approached. "Quick, hide away from us, Sarah."

Sarah swam off into some seaweed to lie low. At that point, Elwin and Lily then began to swim into a school of fish, scattering them noisily out of the garden. The guards saw them, just as Elwin thought. The guards started to swim toward them, and as they approached, Elwin swam from behind his rock to another, allowing himself to become briefly visible. Four dark mermen descended on them, while another held the mermaid. At first Elwin and Lily tried to fight them. Lily even shot the crossbow the elves had given her but missed. The mermen soon surrounded them, and they put up their hands. In a matter of minutes, the mermen had taken their weapons and were escorting them to the grotto.

"Remember what the elves said about the hag," Elwin whispered as they led them away. "Do not eat or drink anything, and beware her voice."

Suddenly, Lily got an idea. She tore small pieces of cloth off the dress she carried in her pack, which she held in front of her. Then she stuffed them in her ears.

Watching all of this from her hiding place, Sarah finally swam up as they entered the cave, creeping carefully after they passed so she would remain unnoticed. Already, Elwin and Lily were standing before the hag, who was questioning them at a table about a dozen yards from her throne.

"And who is this?" the hag asked her guards.

"A mermaid we found hiding from us who needs a lesson," they answered.

"Not her, these others."

"Spies. We caught them sneaking around your gardens outside the cave," one of the dark mermen responded.

"Spies? For who?" the hag asked.

"We had reports from our soldiers fighting the merpeople near the Bermuda Triangle a few days ago that there was an elf with them," the guard replied.

"So, you are spies for King Triton?" she asked Elwin and Lily.

Elwin and Lily said nothing. Seeing that they were unafraid, Hagatha decided to take another tack to put them off their guard.

"You may leave them with me. Take the mermaid into the reception room. The fact that she was hiding when spies were swimming about my lair is very suspicious, but I will deal with her later. Wait until I call for you," she said. Then turning to Elwin and Lily, she continued. "Come. Let us have a talk."

The hag led them into her room, where a table was laid out with various foods and bottles of liquid, sealed against the ocean. "You must be tired and hungry from wandering about my domain. Eat something, and we will talk."

"You are kind," Elwin said, "But we are not hungry. Isn't that right?"

Lily said nothing, but made no motion toward the food or gave even the slightest interest in the foods set before them.

"Please sit, then, and we will talk while I breakfast," Hagatha said.

At first, Elwin started to resist, but thinking he would be better appearing congenial, he sat down, and Lily sat beside him. Sarah continued to watch them from outside the cave.

"I must ask myself, what are an elf and a human child doing in my realm so far in the deep?" she said. "There is something unusual in this, and since I do not speak to surface peoples often, this is a real treat for me." She made it seem like they were doing her a favor, being caught.

"We were simply exploring the ocean floor and got lost," Elwin said. Lily remained mute, and Sarah continued to watch.

"Exploring? Yes, but for whom? And no doubt you got lost in my mines, but you would have had to make it past many defenses and soldiers who would have already captured you. Obviously, you were trying to sneak in, but for what purpose, and for whom?" Hagatha asked.

"Who says that we were exploring for someone besides our own people?" Elwin exclaimed, trying to control the conversation. Yet it was obvious that she could see through his lies, as is usually the case when people try to deceive grownups, especially ones that are witches.

"Come now. Please do not treat me like a fool. I may be old, but I am not doddering." Almost for a moment, Elwin felt a little ashamed at his attempts at deception. "The fact that you are breathing underwater shows me you have been associating with merpeople or others whose magic enables you to even live beneath the surface. The fact that you are here, in the deeps of the Abyss, shows me that Triton's people let you in. Do not bother to argue. His people and mine guard the only entrance to the Abyss. My people would not have let you in, so it must have been his," she said.

Elwin started to deny all connection to the merpeople to protect them, but found the reasoning irresistible. Something in her voice compelled him to answer as she said. "You are right, of course. We came with Triton's people, who told us the way." Sarah winced as she listened. How could he tell on the merpeople? It had to be the hag's spell.

"And what is his purpose? Was he trying to learn about the numbers of my army or when we would attack?" Hagatha asked.

Again, Elwin tried to resist, but ended up saying, "No. In fact, until we came, neither he nor his people were aware that you had built such a large army or that you had another way out than the crack of the Abyss. We had planned on telling him."

"We will see about that. What, then, was his ultimate goal? What is his strategy?" Hagatha asked.

Elwin tried to resist and avoid giving too much away. He could not refuse to answer, but he tried to answer only partially to try to throw her off the scent. "I have never seen or met him. He sent Lily, here, and I accompanied her. Some of his people came with her as well. I do not know his ultimate plan or strategy concerning you. Only that he sent us and that his real purpose is against the Sand Wizard, who is also the enemy of my people."

"The Sand Wizard? Ah yes. That makes sense. He cannot fight on two fronts, so he was trying to end the war with me. Well, I will have to let the Sand Wizard know to accelerate our plans, and Triton will find himself surrounded much faster than he expected," Hagatha said to Elwin. As she spoke, she turned to nod toward the largest mirror that hung on the wall.

It must be some kind of communications device, Elwin thought

"My dear," Hagatha said to Lily, touching her hand, "What is the purpose to which Triton sent you? What is his strategy?"

Lily said nothing, and Sarah continued to watch.

"Why have you come?" she asked again.

Again, Lily did not reply.

"What information are you trying to get?" she asked, her voice rising in volume.

Lily continued to stare forward, and Sarah sat watching.

"You will tell me now why Triton sent you!" she said, getting angry and wondering why the girl did not answer. It was unusual for anyone to resist so long, especially this little girl.

Still, Lily sat stone-faced. Hagatha stood up and jerked Lily up from her chair, holding her by her shoulders and looking her in the eye.

"Either you tell me the plans of Triton, or I will take you to the mines to work forever!" she yelled in Lily's face.

"La, la, la, I am not listening," Lily said, pointing to her ears, her ear plugs now visible for the first time.

"Aaargh," Hagatha screamed, as the spell was broken. Suddenly, her voice no longer held Elwin in its sway. Her anger had destroyed the influence of her magic, which lasted only as long as she seemed reasonable and helpful. They both saw her for what she was.

"Now," Elwin yelled.

Sarah darted in from the ledge, swimming as hard as she could. She grabbed the trident, turned, and pushing off the wall started to swim back out, but some of the dark mermen blocked her way. Two others held the mermaid, who floated compliantly between their arms.

"Shelly, help me," Sarah said.

Shelly did not move.

"If you want your freedom, now is the time!" Sarah cried, as the dark mermen were closing in.

"I cannot disobey. You must set me free," she replied.

"I forgot," Sarah said. Then holding the trident in front of her in imitation of the hag and staring at Shelly, she said, "I release you from all commands. You no longer need to obey the guards or work in the mines. You are free."

Immediately, Shelly pulled loose of the dark mermen and darted into the room next to Sarah. She fanned her tail and slapped it in the face of one of the advancing guards, releasing bubbles as she did. Seeing an opening where the merman was standing, Sarah darted through and out into the cavern with Shelly on her heels. The other mermen soon followed.

Hagatha, on realizing that another human child had stolen the trident before she could react, turned on Elwin and Lily and shouted, "Thieves!"

As she said this, her tail seemed to unwind and became eight arms like an octopus, though whether it was through some magic or whether she was born with this mutation and had hidden it all this time they did not know. She swam toward them, grabbing the three knives off the table in different arms, while holding a scepter in her human hands.

"It matters not that you kill us," Elwin said. "Sarah has taken the trident, and there is nothing you can do to stop her. Now you will lose your kingdom."

Hagatha stopped dead in the water. "You are wrong. There is something I can do." Then turning to the two mermen who had let Shelly go, she instructed them, "Kill the thieves," pointing at Elwin and Lily.

The mermen swam at them with their spears. Elwin rushed one of the mermen, and Lily tried to move so that the stone columns were between her and the other. Meanwhile, with them occupied, Hagatha turned her back on them and stood in front of the mirror.

"Somnambulus," she said. The mirror started to swirl different colors. "Triton has sent spies into my realm. They have discovered our attack plans and are escaping. Seal the way out from our secret tunnel. We will ensure they cannot escape through the gates."

Elwin, who was wrestling with one of the mermen over his spear and hearing what she said into the mirror, stripped the spear from his hands and threw it at the hag. She moved out of the way, and the spear struck the mirror, cracking it. The colors in the mirror blinked, and then it went black.

"Aargh," Hagatha yelled again, as she advanced toward them.

Lily, however, was already darting out of the grotto. The other merman was in pursuit until Elwin caught him by surprise and knocked him into a column. Grabbing his and Lily's weapons from the dazed guard, he then sped past him and out into the cavern. Knowing they could not hide from their pursuers, the two swam as fast as they could. The merman was soon behind them, but they would make it to the tunnel long before he got to them and would be gone.

Suddenly, the whole cavern started to shake and rocks fell from the ceiling. They made it to the tunnel, but advancing down it was a host of the dark mermen. They looked back, trying to seek some escape. There were several other caves entering the garden, but rocks were falling in several of them, and the mermen were coming out of others like ants from an anthill. They could see Hagatha standing on the ledge before her grotto, laughing maniacally. They were trapped, and Sarah was nowhere to be seen.

"We must make our stand," Elwin said, as he and Lily got their crossbows ready.

# 16

# The Slave Revolt

Sarah swam across the grotto and down one of the tunnels, with Shelly on her heels and a half dozen dark mermen on Shelly's.

"Let me lead," Shelly said as she swam in front of Sarah, who paused only a second before taking off after her.

Immediately, Shelly took a left, a right, another left, then another left. Sarah quickly lost track of where they were going, but so did the mermen, who, because they were much farther behind, were soon out of sight. One of the advantages of being a slave in the mines was that Shelly had a much greater knowledge of the tunnels than her overseers, who came and went and knew only a much smaller area of the mines. Since the mermen who followed were royal guards and not slave guards, they knew even less. Within minutes, Sarah and Shelly had lost them.

Still, Shelly kept on, barely pausing to allow Sarah to see which way she had gone. It was several minutes later when Shelly stopped. She held out a hand to keep Sarah from swimming into a large cavern. After she stopped, Sarah saw why. It was an enormous cavern beehived with tunnels running this way and that. In the center was a large group of merpeople with a line of dark mermen around the edges to keep them from escaping.

"What are you doing?" Sarah asked. "Why don't we lead them in throwing off their bonds?"

"For the same reason I did not help you at first," Shelly said.

"You mean because I have not ordered their freedom and they are still under the spell of the witch," Sarah responded.

"Correct," Shelly replied.

"But certainly I can order their freedom now," Sarah stated.

"Yes, but what do you think the hag's servants will do if you swim into their midst and raise *her* trident over *your* head?" Shelly asked.

"I had not thought of that. So what do we do?" Sarah asked.

"I will have to distract them," Shelly explained. "I will go into the cavern first and draw the guards away. Wait until they are all at one end of the cavern, and then go in the midst of the slaves and wish them free."

Without waiting for Sarah to object, Shelly swam out into the cavern and started mingling with the other merpeople, whispering to them. Sarah assumed she was giving them instructions.

"You, there," one of the mermen said, "what are you doing talking to the other prisoners? Come here, at once."

Shelly swam up to the dark merman docilely, but then suddenly threw sand into his eyes. She then started swimming across the cavern as fast as she could.

"Stop, there! Come back!" the merman said. "Hagatha's spell must have worn off. Quick, get her!"

All of the dark mermen chased after her until they were far across the cavern. Sarah immediately charged out of the tunnel. She could see the mermen closing in on Shelly, tridents in hand. In a minute, they would be in range to capture her or, worse, to stab her. She had to work quickly.

A few seconds later, Sarah was in the midst of the slave merpeople. She raised the trident over her head and said, "Through the power of Triton, I hereby release you from the hag's commands and from obedience to her people or other slaves. You are free to follow your own orders."

As soon as she started to speak, the dark mermen stopped and looked. As soon as they saw Sarah, they started to swim back, except for the one merman who had originally started chasing Shelly. It was enough, for Shelly quickly turned and faced her opponent. Meanwhile, the other mermen soon faced a host of merpeople. Sarah thought at first that they would simply flee, but she soon saw she was wrong. The hag's people were used to intimidating others using force. They tried the same tactic, and when the slaves did not back down, they proceeded to attack. The merpeople had to fight hard against the mermen using the pick axes, shovels, and even rocks to attack their former guards.

In a few minutes, it was all over. Four of the slaves were dead, stabbed by tridents or spears. But all but two of the guards were dead or wounded. These two had fled. The one merman that faced Shelly was one of these. Shelly had evaded him and, when faced with the crowd, he swam off down one of the tunnels. The crowd started to cheer.

"Wait, we must move now against the witch," Sarah said.

"She is right," Shelly agreed. "The hag will not give up so easily when she has a whole army behind her. Her troops will try to get us back under control. We must quickly cut her off from her troops to prevent their attack. Then we need to get out of here."

"We need more merpeople," Sarah said.

"Let us move to the other two large caverns and free the slaves in them also," Shelly said.

So they swam down another twisting and turning tunnel until they came to another cavern, where they followed a similar plan to distract the guards and release the slaves, only this time they had a whole army of merpeople with them to help. By the time they got to the second cavern mentioned by Shelly, they met a crowd unguarded by the dark mermen.

"They swam off after they got word about some elf queen swimming around releasing the slaves," one of the merpeople told them.

"Hah! Elf queen," Sarah said.

"Good, that makes it easier," Shelly said.

Sarah then spoke, holding the trident in front of her. "By the power of Triton, I hereby release all of you from the hag's spell. You are free to disobey and leave and choose your own destinies."

Backed by this large army, Sarah and Shelly headed back to the sea hag's grotto. As they did, the tunnel started to quake, and stones fell from the ceiling. Despite the danger, they did not shrink back but kept going forward. They ran into dark mermen once, but the hag's small number of runners and guards in the tunnel fled before the mass of merpeople or else from the earthquakes. In only minutes, the former slaves streamed into the grotto through a tunnel entrance.

There in the midst of the cavern swam Lily and Elwin, surrounded by the dark mermen, who were also entering the cave from all directions. Lily and Elwin shot their crossbows, and two or three of the mermen fell, but given the hundreds they now faced, it made no difference. They would soon be overwhelmed no matter how they fought. Still, there was no thought of surrender. They both knew that the only alternatives were enslavement or death.

Suddenly, a mass of merpeople came flooding into the grotto. These were of many different hues and colors, not the pale skin and dark hair of the hag's mermen. Leading them were Sarah and Shelly.

In an instant, the battle changed. A wedge of merpeople quickly split in two the mass of mermen surrounding Lily and Elwin. Soon they had pushed through to rescue them. Other than a few stragglers, there were now two enemy lines: One blocked the way to the hag, and the other blocked the way out.

"Come," Elwin shouted. "They are too many! Focus on freeing yourselves. To the tunnel!"

The mass of freed slaves ignored the hag and pushed toward the tunnel, while a rear guard protected the group from those behind them. The fight was dreadful. The girls saw many on both sides fall into the vegetation below them, but the merpeople had the advantage of a divided enemy. They soon pushed their way to the tunnel. For some way into the tunnel, the fighting continued, but the dark mermen finally fled before them leaving the way open.

As the freed slaves pushed forward, they occasionally ran into groups of slaves asking to be freed, and Sarah quickly released them to join the uprising. In the distance, across large caverns or down side tunnels, they saw the slaves fighting the dark mermen. The revolt was spreading as more and more of the merpeople threw off the yokes of the hag and picked up arms against their former masters. Yet the girls and the large group of merpeople led by Shelly continued to push forward through the tunnel toward the entrance to the mines and the Abyss.

The earthquakes, meanwhile, continued, and falling rocks struck both the slaves and the guards pursuing them. It was not long before the dark mermen gave up because of the danger, and the freed merpeople seemed to meet no more resistance.

Finally, the group came to the side tunnel leading steadily upward.

"Quick, this way!" Elwin said.

"But the entrance is this way," one of the merpeople argued.

"We would never make it out of the Abyss, let alone through the front gate. Besides, the hag said she was sending her troops to block our way out," Lily said.

"Does this tunnel go to the surface, as I believe?" Elwin asked.

"Yes, but it comes out far into the hag's territory," another answered.

"We will have to take that risk," Elwin said.

They turned to the right and started making the ascent up the tunnel. It was very steep in some places, appearing more like a well or shaft extending upwards a dozen yards or more, like a ladder or stairs. At other places, the incline was more gradual, a straight, smooth road leading to the surface. As they neared the ocean floor, the tunnel became rougher and narrower, with more rock formations, lower ceilings, and unfinished surfaces.

At first, as they went on, the rear guard occasionally skirmished with the dark mermen pursuing them. The dark mermen would approach, and the last few of the former slaves would stop to fight while the rest moved on. Then the guards would retreat. One or two freed slaves had fallen to their tridents, but many more of the dark mermen had received injuries or death. Yet as earthquakes and tremors continued to increase, and rocks started falling from the ceiling, their pursuers fell farther and farther behind. By the time the group reached the roughest part of the tunnel, all pursuit had ended.

"The earthquake must be the work of the Sand Wizard," Sarah said. "Based on what Ishmael said, I think this is beyond the witch's power, but it seems directly in line with what we know the Sand Wizard can do, even though he is far away."

"Do you think he knows we are here?" Lily asked.

"Probably not," Elwin replied. "The earthquakes seem pretty general in their target. That is, he is not causing specific tunnels to collapse. He only shakes the entire area."

Still, they went on and on. Finally, the tunnel became so narrow and twisted, they could only proceed in single file. This was particularly hazardous because of the tremors, for there was now no room in the tunnel to avoid falling rocks. The tunnel itself now took different turns and branches, so that they were afraid they might get lost and not choose the right tunnel leading out.

Sarah and Shelly swam ahead to make sure the tunnel was clear and to scout out the way forward. It was while these two were ahead of the rest that another tremor struck, and rock began to fall from the ceiling directly on them. They tried to bolt ahead, but even more rock fell on them. Instinctively, Sarah grabbed the necklace she had found in Atlantis. Shelly, who feared for the human's life, tucked her head and wrapped herself around Sarah, hoping to shield her from the worst of the rock. Amazingly, no rocks fell directly on them, but the stones seemed to pile up around them until they were in a small hole in the very midst of the piles of rock.

"What did you do?" Shelly asked.

"It's this necklace I got from a little girl in Atlantis," Sarah replied. "It must protect the wearer by providing some kind of shield. It is almost like the fairies left this behind for me to find for just such a moment as this."

"Well, we are safe," Shelly said, "But we are trapped."

"All we can do is wait for the others to dig us out," Sarah said.

That is exactly what the others were doing. When the tunnel collapsed in front of them, at first Elwin pulled Lily back to protect her. The other merpeople backed down the tunnel and tried to shield themselves under rock outcroppings or ledges. Suddenly, Lily realized that Sarah and Shelly were still ahead, directly under where the rocks had fallen.

"Sarah!" she cried, and rushed forward, even as the debris was still settling. She tried to find a way forward, but the tunnel was completely blocked. She then tried to start moving stones in an attempt to open up the tunnel and find her sister, but it was a somewhat random attempt and not very effective.

"The tunnel has completely collapsed," Elwin said. "Quick, we must rescue Sarah and Shelly."

"It is too late for them. We must save ourselves," one merman said. "Perhaps we can go back around to the main entrance to the Abyss?"

"We would never get out that way," said another, who swam up from behind. "Besides, the tunnel is also blocked by rubble behind us."

"Aye, but not as much," said a third. "There looks like a gap at the top. We have a much better chance of getting out that way than ahead."

"Maybe," said Elwin, "But if we have no chance of getting out through the gate, it makes little difference. Besides, we must try to rescue the girls or at least recover what remains. We must try to get out through the tunnel, if at all possible. At the very least, we can see how difficult it will be. If we cannot get out that way, we will go back the other way."

The merpeople agreed and started to clear the rock from the tunnel ahead. At first, they discarded the rocks to the sides because they did not want to seal off the tunnel behind them, but when they ran out of room, they started to pile the rock on the debris blocking the way back. They made quick progress because of the number of people moving rocks, and the long chains of merpeople helped them to get the rocks out of the way. At the very front of the line, lifting heavy rocks, were Elwin and Lily.

Soon, Sarah and Shelly heard the digging. "We are here!" they yelled.

In another few minutes, Elwin and Lily had made a hole where Sarah and Shelly were.

"It's a miracle you were not crushed," Elwin said. "We will have you out in mere minutes."

The group soon pulled out a few more stones, carefully removing the rock on top of them first, until the girls were united again.

"How much farther down the tunnel did it collapse?" a merman asked.

"I don't know. Not far, I think," Shelly replied.

They set to it moving more rock in front of them while blocking off the tunnel behind. They did not clear all of the rock; it was just too much. But they were able to clear a path through it until they reached open tunnel ahead.

"Well, at least we know we will not be followed that way," said Elwin, looking back at the pile of rock behind them some fifty feet thick. "At least not for some time."

"Right," Shelly said. "Best to go quickly."

The group entered the last stage of the tunnel. They could tell from the water pressure that they were not as deep now. After another burst of swimming, they saw light ahead. In another minute, they exited the tunnel. They were finally free of the Abyss.

# 17

# The Surface Again

When Elwin, Sarah, Lily, and the freed merpeople emerged from the tunnel, they were in a small outpost on an outcropping of rock some hundred feet above the ocean floor. Seaweed camouflaged the tunnel entrance, and a roof of stone and coral covered both the tunnel and the fort. Four dark mermen manned the fort, but as soon as they saw such a large host of slaves emerge instead of the army they were expecting, they fled.

"Well, we are out of the tunnel and in a better position than we were, but we are by no means free from danger," Elwin said.

"What do we do?" Lily asked.

"We must get back to the towers of the Abyss, where Barracuda is waiting for us," Sarah said.

"Which way is it?" Shelly asked.

"That way," Lily said, pointing, "I think."

They took off swimming *en masse*, watching for any movement. They expected at any time for the armies of the hag to swim out to meet them, or at least to see her scouts swimming off to warn her main forces. However, they saw no one and nothing, not a fish or octopus, throughout the lands south of the Abyss that the hag called her domain.

"This is very unexpected," Elwin said. "Her troops must be distracted by something."

"Perhaps they are still looking for us," Sarah said.

"Maybe, but I think we had best approach the Abyss carefully. Let's take a wide berth to the east and approach the towers from the north," Elwin advised.

The other mermen seemed to agree, so they headed east over some mountains to an even deeper part of the ocean. They did not swim along the bottom but maintained a fairly even depth, even though this might make them visible to spies. Part of the reason they did not go deeper was that all of them, the merpeople included, missed the surface and the light and did not want to return to the depths anytime soon. They made a wide bend, going out into the ocean until the mountains on the east side of the Abyss looked small, then they swam north until they could no longer see the mountains, and then finally they headed back to where they thought the Abyss should be. It took them several hours to follow this route, so that it was getting dark when they finally saw the Abyss as they approached from the north.

What the merpeople saw amazed them. There was a full-blown war ongoing. All along the Abyss, they could see large lights in the towers and smaller lights spread out along both edges, signs that there were troops amassed. As they got closer, they could see missiles of various types being launched from the towers into the assembled armies – tridents and spears, crossbow bolts, and flaming globs, which they later learned was Greek fire or phosphorus, which burned even brighter under water than above. Occasionally, they saw lines of soldiers move, attack in close quarters, and then retreat.

"Well, now we know what was distracting the dark mermen," Elwin said.

At first, it seemed as if King Triton's people were winning. They not only held the line but made several successful assaults, pushing the hag's mermen behind their own towers and even into the hills beyond. But then at the last moment of daylight a stream of new mermen flooded from out of the Abyss and drove back the merpeople to their own side of the crevasse. They only beat back this new assault because the attacks from Triton's towers were so fierce that the dark mermen could not pass them without heavy losses. As night set in, they retreated to their own side of the Abyss and settled in for dawn, leaning against the rocks next to their tridents and setting out lanterns to see the enemy coming.

Meanwhile, Sarah, Lily, Elwin, Shelly, and the rest of the merpeople, numbering several hundred, continued to approach the Abyss from the north. They now kept low to the ground and worked their way through several narrow canyons along the ocean floor, moving steadily toward the towers.

"Halt, who goes there!" a sentry demanded, as they approached a turn in one canyon. A young merman swam out from behind a rock. He held his trident before him. "Do not proceed any farther unless you wish for certain death. A dozen warriors are only a shout away."

"It is the human children and the elf only just escaped from the hag's lair. We must see Barracuda at once," Elwin said.

"Barracuda is leading the assault. I have heard of no such developments, nor has anyone said that human children would be coming this way. And who are these others?" the sentry asked.

"They are escaped slaves from the mines of the hag. No doubt Barracuda was expecting us to come from the Abyss and did not warn anyone watching his rear. Nevertheless, we speak the truth. Go, send a messenger to him and see what response you get. But be quick. Our business with him is urgent, and the battle may depend on our seeing him," Elwin said.

The youth retreated behind the rocks once more. It took a good half hour, with the girls and mass of merpeople waiting patiently. Finally, the sentry swam out once again, this time with his weapons lowered.

"Come forward and enter. My apologies for the delay, but I had to be sure. Barracuda himself is coming to meet you," the sentry said.

"We do not blame you," Elwin said, "For you are only doing as a good sentry should."

The mass of merpeople passed into the camp. For a quarter of a mile behind the towers, there were small squads of mermen bedded down together or sitting in circles eating or talking quietly. In some places, the circles were very close together, and the merpeople were as thick as flies. The newcomers moved between the camps as well as they could, heading toward the towers. Suddenly, a familiar figure approached carrying a lantern. It was Barracuda.

"Elwin, Sarah, Lily! I cannot say how glad I am to see you. When the hag started the attack, I could only believe you were dead or had no chance of escaping. You must tell me how you came to approach us from the rear, but first, who are these others?" Barracuda asked.

"We are escaped slaves, whom Sarah set free and the others helped escape," Shelly said. "We have come to join in the war, for we have a grudge against this hag."

"You are most welcome," Barracuda said. "Seek out Hammerhead, the armorer. He will give you proper weapons. Then join the others and get some food. I see among you some military men I had thought dead. They can help to organize and prepare you for battle.

"Now," he continued, "Sarah, Lily, and Elwin, please join me. I wish to hear your tale, but let us go somewhere where we may sit quietly."

Barracuda led them to the base of a tower. A sentry opened the door for them, spilling out a warm yellow light, and they passed inside. The light inside was brilliant from many lanterns on the walls. They swam up a shaft to a room high up in the tower. A trapdoor in the ceiling led into the top, where they could see above them instruments of war lying ready. In the chamber which they entered, they could see chairs, a table with food prepared, and Scallop seated at the table.

"Sarah! Lily!" she said, getting up and swimming to them. They embraced her as an old friend. Soon they were all seated at the table and stuffing themselves.

Once they were refreshed, Barracuda said, "Now, tell me the tale. But be brief."

It was mostly Elwin who talked, with Sarah adding in those parts of the tale that Elwin did not know. Along the way, he described the encounters they had, the number of forces, the weapon systems, and the layout of the hag's lair, such things as an experienced soldier might want to know. Barracuda was particularly interested in the tunnel.

"So that is how her people came to be so far from the Abyss!" he exclaimed.

"Well, the good news is that it will take some time for her to clear that way because of the earthquakes she herself requested," Elwin said. "I can show you exactly where the entrance is on a map, and you can take the appropriate action to close it off permanently."

"There is another thing that answers a lot of questions," Barracuda said. "For a long time, it has appeared as though the hag and the Sand Wizard's actions were coordinated and that they were in league, yet we knew of no communication between them, for we would have seen the messengers come and go. Now, we know for sure."

When they came to the part of the tale where Sarah stole the trident, Barracuda stopped them. "So you were successful in getting Triton's trident? Where is it?"

Sarah took out a cloth which she had wrapped around the trident after they had made it out of the caves. She unwrapped it, and there it was in her hand – a golden trident decorated with silver scallops. Barracuda took it gently in his hands.

"This is most unexpected after the day that we had. When the armies attacked midday, we feared you were dead, for why would the witch attack prematurely unless she had discovered you, and how could you get out of the Abyss with her soldiers swimming all around? We had all but given up hope, and now you have escaped and have completed your quest. It is almost too good to be true," Barracuda said.

"So what is next?" Elwin asked.

Just at that moment, the five of them heard shouts from above, and a hail of missiles clicked against the outer stones of the tower. It suddenly became very light outside the windows as the merpeople dumped Greek fire on enemy forces below.

"It is another sortie," Barracuda said. He swam up to the top of the tower and started directing the soldiers there to fire on the enemy. The enemy fired back, even launching some missile or stone that shook the very walls of the lower chamber where the girls sat. They crouched down under the table just in case. After about ten minutes the clamor died, and the enemy retreated. Barracuda swam back down after another few minutes.

"That was quick," Elwin said.

"They were only testing the defenses, to see if there were weaknesses or if our people were not alert," Barracuda responded.

"We have no time to lose," he added. "If we are to end this battle and prepare to strike at the Sand Wizard, we must get the trident to Triton. Only then can he command the seas and stop the hag."

"What must we do, then?" Sarah inquired.

"You... you must proceed with the mission Triton gave you and distract the Sand Wizard by facing him at his lair," Barracuda replied.

"But what about the trident?" Lily asked.

"Someone else must take it to Triton. This is a mission that calls for speed, and although you may be very fine swimmers for your kind, you would not have the speed or endurance of a merman and would take many more days. No, I shall take the trident," Barracuda said.

"But you cannot go," Scallop said. "Who will lead the armies? Who will defeat the hag?"

"If the trident does not get into Trident's hands, we can hold off the hag but never really defeat her. Getting the trident to him is the most important task. I said it would take speed, but it will also take discretion. Who else can we trust with such an important weapon, who would not lose it, steal it, or let it fall into the hands of the enemy? No, I dare not trust another with such an important task. There are other generals who can lead the assault."

"What about me?" Scallop asked.

"You must go with the children and ensure they get to the wizard's castle," Barracuda said. "Again, in this case, I must be the one to carry the trident. Now, if you will excuse me. We only have a few more hours until daylight, and I must make preparations for departing. You will need to also get some sleep, for you have a long journey to start tomorrow."

After a few more minutes of protest, the children finally gave in to Barracuda's request, but it took Elwin talking to them later to see the wisdom in what he proposed. Barracuda left to make preparations for them while they themselves doused the lights and finally lay down in the underwater cocoons used by the merpeople as sleeping bags. They found that they were very much tired and ready for bed. Elwin pointed out that, not counting the uneasy naps in the mines, the last real sleep they had was in Atlantis three nights before. They had been so busy with their task, they had not noticed they had gotten almost no sleep.

"Do you think they will attack again?" Lily asked as they were drifting off to sleep.

Sarah was going to reassure her, but Lily was already snoring before she could answer, and she was asleep herself before she could think to herself that it was not very polite to ask a question and fall asleep before getting the answer.

Sarah never did find out the answer to Lily's question. They slept so soundly, the whole of the hag's army could have attacked and they would not have known it. They did not awaken until Barracuda shook them before dawn.

"It is still dark," Lily said.

"Yes, we must get on the way before our enemy knows we have gone, for they will surely plan another attack if they know I am not here," Barracuda said.

"I hope that you got a little rest," Elwin said.

"A few hours, which is enough to get me back to Coral. But I had much to do before I could retire," he replied.

It took a few minutes for Sarah, Lily, and Scallop to get their things together, and then they grabbed a quick breakfast in the tower room. But they had no time for leisure. Barracuda continued to push them out the door, so that finally they left, with Sarah still trying to spread some jellyfish jelly on her bit of sea cucumber.

The five of them swam to the edge of camp, and then mounted a manta ray, which helped them get moving quickly. As the girls were all still very sleepy, they could sit on the ray and rest. Barracuda guided the ray past the sentry and out of the camp. By the time the sun began to shine down through the water, they were well north of the camp. They could see the Abyss and the towers, but they were very distant. Barracuda seemed to relax a little, knowing that they had escaped unseen.

They continued for at least another hour until they came to a ridge. Barracuda guided them over a few hills until he found a cove hidden in the rocks and surrounded by coral. They dismounted the ray and swam into it. There they found, hidden beneath some seaweed, a small coracle, a little boat like a canoe, with several heavy rocks in it. It was tied down to stakes in the sandy bottom in four places.

"This is where we part," Barracuda said. "You and Scallop must take the boat to the surface, while I go on by myself toward Coral with the trident."

"Why don't the girls stop and finish eating the breakfast they started, and we can uncover the boat," Elwin said.

They all agreed, and in a few minutes, he and Barracuda had the rocks out of the boat and their baggage loaded within it. The girls finished eating, and then sat in the boat.

"Better strap yourselves in," Barracuda suggested.

The girls found ropes with which to tie themselves to the seats.

"Oh, don't forget the trident," Sarah said, handing it to Barracuda.

"I would have been angry with myself if I had forgotten that," he said, taking it. "Scallop knows the way back to the beach and the sandcastle. Now, I must go. I still have a long swim to go and a long war with the hag before I can rest again."

Barracuda took the package, still wrapped up in case someone saw him, and then he took off toward the north. As the others settled in, Elwin took his knife and cut the first rope. A corner of the boat jerked upwards. He cut the second rope, and the front of the boat tipped up. He handed the knife to Scallop, who cut the third rope, and the boat swiveled around, hanging by the last remaining rope.

"Hold on!" he cried as Scallop cut the last rope. The boat started to plunge toward the surface. It was a wild ride as the boat flipped from side to side, all the while whizzing through the water. Scallop swam below them. They could see her swimming as fast as she could and still falling behind. They passed the cliffs leading to the continental shelf, but continued up at a rapid pace. After a few more minutes, they could see the surface approaching. It came faster and faster, a flat level plane, lit by the sunlight.

Suddenly, the boat emerged from the water in a rush and roar of water as they flew above the surface. They landed again with a splash. There was the sunlight and the waves and a breeze coming from the east. The sunlight and air felt good on their skin.

They started to breathe a sigh of relief, yet for some reason, they found they could not breathe at all. It was like their lungs were not working. They gasped for air. Suddenly, Sarah realized what it was. They were still under the spell of the mermaid. They would drown above the surface if they could not get below water again. She wanted to tell the others, but no air was in her body to speak the words. She tried to untie the rope, but it was wet, and the knot was hard to work. Lily, being skinnier, slipped out from under her rope as soon as she also realized the same thing. She was then in the water. A few seconds later, Sarah had her rope undone. She looked, but realized that Elwin, who tied a much harder knot, could not undo his. He was too large to wiggle out. She looked around for their knife, but realized that Scallop still had it.

Quickly, she dove into the water. She looked around, and there was Scallop swimming up with the knife, all tuckered out. Sarah said, "Quick! Give me the knife."

Scallop gave it to her, and she pushed out of the water and onto the boat, cut the rope, and then pulled Elwin, who was nearly unconscious, into the water. After another few seconds, they were all revived and alert again.

"I remembered the spell after I cut the last rope, but I could not catch up with you," Scallop said. She swam around the girls, splashing them with bubbles. Then she kissed them all. They climbed back out onto the boat, able to breathe at last.

"Finally, we are back on the surface again," Elwin said. Even though he was enamored by the sea, he was glad to return to the sky and the world that he knew after so many days underwater.

# 18

## The Tidal Pool

The girls and Elwin got into the little coracle, which was rounded like a small canoe, and then started to take turns rowing until Elwin found a sail and mast in the bottom and put them up. The girls were still not very good at sailing, but Elwin showed them how. He helped them practice tacking to keep the wind at their backs and gave them many pointers. After a few lessons, the girls finally got the hang of it and were able to sail the boat while Elwin took his turn resting.

Scallop, meanwhile, swam along beside the boat, giving them directions as they went, but mostly she talked to Sarah and Lily, asking them questions about what had happened to them in the Abyss.

"What was the name of the mermaid you met in the hag's mines?" she asked them.

"Shelly," Lily responded.

"Shelly? That was the name of a mermaid I knew many years ago. We actually schooled together, but she did not return from summer vacation one year. I always thought she moved. Now I suppose I know better, if indeed it is the same person. I would like to see her again someday."

"We never did hear what happened to you and Barracuda while we were gone," Sarah said.

"At first, nothing happened," Scallop replied. "We left you at the tunnel coming from Atlantis and snuck up the side of the Abyss. Because of the dark mermen watching from the towers on the other side, it was a little dangerous. We kept to the shadows, and Barracuda knew a path behind some rocks that took us out of sight until we made it to one of the towers.

"Once there, Barracuda took charge and started ordering the defenses. He thought all along that the hag would attack if she discovered you. He was right, of course, although I did not see at first what that meant. He seemed to have little hope that you would make it out undiscovered. Actually, he later said that he did not think you would make it back at all. I thought he was being pessimistic, but he said in his serious manner, 'I do not think, but I hope against all that I know.'

"Soon after we arrived, he sent a swimmer to request back up soldiers from Coral, and they arrived the morning of the next day. We were waiting the whole time. It was pretty boring. I tried to look at some maps of the Abyss and guess where you were, but after that, there was not a whole lot to do. The only consolation was that the food was good after being out in the ocean, and I was able to get a lot of sleep, for I fell asleep several times waiting.

"About midday the day after the soldiers arrived, we noticed a lot of movement on the other side of the Abyss," Shelly continued. "There were a lot of lights in the towers, and dark mermen were making camp behind the towers. Barracuda thought that could only mean one thing, that you had been discovered. He started to organize our people, you know, spreading them along the line behind the towers, making sure everyone had weapons, and then coordinating with the other towers. About midafternoon, the dark mermen started to launch missiles from their towers, driving our people behind sheltered rocks. Then they attacked. We drove them back several times, but the fighting was heavy. It was only when Barracuda ordered the use of the Greek fire that we were able to disperse them."

"What is Greek fire?" Sarah asked.

"It is an ancient concoction developed by the Greeks many thousands of years ago," Scallop said. "Basically, it is a mixture of tar and phosphorus that sticks to things and burns. Because of the oil and the phosphorus, it is one of the few fires that will burn in the water. We learned about it when our ancestors helped the Greeks fight the Persian War, but we have little of it because it is difficult to get the materials. We have to go on land to get it most of the time, so it costs us dearly, but it is a fierce weapon.

"We only had enough of the stuff to fend off a couple of charges, and by the time that you came we had pretty much used up our stores. Luckily, it was dark by then, and although the dark mermen can see better at night than we can because they are used to swimming in the Abyss, their slaves can't, and they use their slaves heavily in the towers to bring them supplies. So, they pulled back after sundown. I really expected them to attack again at night, but perhaps they were waiting for reinforcements, or maybe the hag thought she would recover the trident, which she could use to wipe us out in one fell swoop. Anyway, you know the rest," Scallop concluded.

"Perhaps we had better rest for the night," Elwin suggested. "We will have to take turns watching the sail."

They all agreed that Sarah would take the first watch, Elwin the second, and Lily the third. Scallop would tie herself with a rope in the boat and be pulled along behind, so as to keep up with them. Once that was settled, they broke out some of the food that Barracuda had packed for them, which was mostly fish, sea cucumbers, and seaweed, all prepared as merpeople delicacies – in other words, they were uncooked but heavily seasoned. Sarah and Lily also ate some snacks out of their bags, such as nuts and raisins, which they had kept dry in sealed bags. There was a jug of freshwater, which Barracuda had sent someone to fetch especially for them, but they had to drink this sparingly because there was not enough to last them their entire journey.

After eating, Elwin and Lily tried to find a comfortable place to catch a few hours of sleep, while Sarah watched the boat. Lily found some plastic floats in the boat, which she blew up to use as a pillow. Elwin lay down in the bottom of the boat, using a jacket as a pillow. Sarah watched the sail, making adjustments as Elwin taught her. Around midnight, Elwin roused and took over the watch.

The next day, the girls awoke, and Elwin was watching the sail while talking to Scallop. Lily had evidently gotten up for a while in the middle of the night to watch the sail, but Elwin could not sleep and had let her lie down again.

The three of them spent several days in this manner, taking turns sleeping and eating and watching the sail. There was not a lot to do on the boat, so they got more than enough rest. The only time they could not sleep was in the heat of the day, and they spent their time talking to Scallop. One afternoon, it rained, and they set out some clothing and bags to catch the rainwater, which they could then drink, but the rest of the time all they saw was fair weather. This was a little surprising to Sarah and Lily, who remembered the storm they had left behind. This was, they thought, the result of magic of some kind, like the fairy magic that made time seem to pass slowly.

About noon on the third day, Sarah, Lily, and Elwin finally saw land ahead of them, just a tiny strip visible only when they were at the top of a wave. It was very distant, several miles at least. They started to make for it, and, drawn in by the tide, made good time.

All the while, Scallop was guiding them. "Go a little more to the left," she would say, or "make for just right of that little inlet."

As they got closer to their destination, the landscape seemed very different than Sarah and Lily remembered. Gone was the hotel where they stayed, or at least it was so far in the background they could not see it. The beach seemed more or less the same, with the same dunes and grass in the background, and the wooden walkway back to the street far behind. More prominent was the sandcastle, which seemed much larger, more elaborate, and more detailed and realistic than the girls remembered it.

"It is time for you to complete the remainder of your journey," Scallop told them. "Unfortunately, I cannot go with you, for the circle of protection made by the Sand Wizard prevents the merpeople from approaching unless under his power. I will stay here and watch the boat. You will need to get to shore and make your way into the castle and seek out the prisoners to help them escape. Beyond this, I cannot provide any guidance, but since you built the castle, you should know the way."

"Yes, but the castle seems very different now," Sarah said. "I think the wizard made his own changes to what we built."

"How are we going to get into the castle when we are so big?" Lily asked.

"I think now is the time to use the last gift of the sea elves," Elwin replied.

"Oh, the potion!" Lily replied. "I had forgotten all about that."

Lily pulled out the little vial the sea elves had given her. They put on their packs so they would shrink, too, and then she, Sarah, and Elwin each took a sip. Lily felt very strange, like she was being folded up like the laundry she did at home. Everything seemed to get bigger. The waves seemed like tidal waves, and the boat seemed a large wooden island. They looked at each other, and they seemed like mice sitting on the seat of the boat. Scallop leaned over the boat to look in, and the entire boat tilted, shifting like an earthquake. She giggled a little as she saw them, for they seemed like the cute little dolls she played with as a fry.

"Great! Now look at us," Elwin squeaked. "Now how will we get to shore? It looks miles and miles away. It's certainly too far to swim the size we are."

"Good thinking, Lily," Sarah said sarcastically.

"Hey, you guys drank it too!" she piped up.

"Do not fear," Scallop said. "I will be right back."

Scallop left them for a while, as the girls repacked their supplies to make for the coast. After a few minutes, she returned carrying a small piece of driftwood. It was about six inches long and slightly concave. She also had several twigs for them to use as oars or a mast.

"That should do nicely," Elwin said. "Thanks, Scallop."

"I think I can make your trip a little shorter," Scallop said. So, she picked them up and placed them in the little boat. Then she carried it and them across the waves until they were several dozen yards closer to shore. Then she gently set them down upon the water.

"This is as close as I can go. I will wait by the boat for you. Take care of yourselves and whatever you do, be safe," Scallop said.

Sarah, Lily, and Elwin set off rowing with the little twigs, getting closer and closer to the shore. Scallop swam back to the boat and was soon out of sight. After they tired of rowing, they made a makeshift sail using their extra shirts and coats, and were able to make a little better time. They sailed or rowed for several hours under the searing sun. As they got closer to shore, they heard the waves crashing from somewhere up ahead.

"I think we have a problem," Elwin said.

"What?" asked Sarah.

"I did not think about it until just now, but we are facing serious danger. I am stupid for not thinking about it after living as a mouse so long, but what do you think the waves are going to look like with us this size?" Elwin asked.

"Uh-oh," Lily said.

The three of them turned to face the shore. Just in front of them, the waves were breaking. They could see the waves to their left and right. It looked like they were falling hundreds of feet.

"Has either one of you ever surfed?" Lily asked.

"No," they replied.

"I saw it in a movie once. We need to come at the waves from the side and try to ride the raft along the inside of the wave. It will take a lot of adjustment to keep it balanced. It would be best to stand up," Lily said.

Sarah looked at Lily in amazement. She really meant to try to surf down what was to them the largest wave of all time, and none of them had ever tried to surf before. Still, Elwin stood and spread out his legs to achieve maximum balance. Sarah and Lily joined him as Sarah realized it was all they could do unless they just hunkered down and rode the wave.

After floating forward for a few minutes, the little piece of driftwood reached the edge of the wave. It was breaking in front of them. Elwin guided their raft along a narrow path, with the wave arching above their heads. They thought they were getting ready to fall when the wave lifted them up. The water crashed over their backs, but they remained upright. A few seconds later, however, they got to the breaker. They rode the wave as before. It seemed they went down a long ways, but they could not say how far. It was Lily who started to lose her balance first. She dove off into the wave and continued to ride it downward. As it turned out, she got way in front of them and the crashing wave. Next it was Elwin.

"Jump off," he cried as he fell off the raft and landed in the water a dozen yards below them.

Sarah tried to obey, but with water all around her, she could not tell which way to jump. She ended up losing her balance as she was tumbling in the water. The raft bumped her head as it went over her, and the water seemed to toss and turn her about until she found her feet on the ground. She stood up. Her head ached, and she was disoriented. She felt the water tugging at her back into deeper water. She had been to the ocean often enough to know what that meant, and she quickly pushed forward as another wave pounded over her head. She woke up she knew not how much later flat on the beach with Lily and Elwin looking over her. All she knew was it was nearly dark. She started to sit up.

"Wait," Elwin told her. "You are lucky to be alive. We pumped the water out of you, and you choked and coughed, so we knew you were alive, but just barely. Are you hurt?"

"My head really hurts, and I feel a little sick when I move," Sarah said.

"Sounds like a concussion," he said. "Better lie still for a little while. The tide has turned and now looks like it is going out. Let us wait until morning before we try to move again. We would not want to enter the castle at night anyway. I will get firewood."

Elwin returned a few minutes later with some driftwood, which he quickly set to light using his woodcraft. They still had some of the fish and other delicacies of the merpeople, but this time they were able to cook them, which was much more to the girls' liking. By the time everything was ready, Sarah was feeling better and sitting up looking around. The sandcastle was not in sight. They must have landed down the beach a ways, she thought.

Sarah, Lily, and Elwin slept right there on the beach, with the fire smoldering beside them. They did not need it for warmth in the summer air, but the thought of having a fire was comforting, for it let them know they were now on land. They looked up at the clear sky and watched the stars. They could see them much easier than at home. It made Sarah glad her father had made her study the constellations. Still, they knew it was dangerous so close to the wizard's castle, even if they saw no evidence of him.

So Elwin sat up watching for a time until early morning, when he woke up Lily. She was cranky, but as she quickly became hungry and got a snack, she was able to stay awake until dawn when she started to stir the others.

The three of them ate a quick breakfast of nuts and raisins, the last of the store that the girls carried, and then set off down the beach. It seemed very different as tiny as they were. The waves were there, but they were much larger. Even the smallest waves seemed to crash well over their heads. The sand was as dusty as usual, but the grains seemed larger and harder when the sand struck them. The sun overhead seemed larger, but it was about as warm as normal for that time and place.

They walked along the beach for some ways until they came to a wide lake, right there on the seashore. Across the lake, they could see a large castle casting its reflection on the still waters. Only instead of gray stone, it was made of yellow sandstone. It was, in fact, their sandcastle, grown to an incredible scale.

"I do not remember this lake being here," Sarah said.

Elwin squatted down, put his hand in the water, and brought it up to his mouth. "It is not a lake. It is a tidal pool. Here, taste. It is brackish."

"There was a low area in front of the castle, but it was way out in the water, with a sandbar on the far side," Lily said.

"I believe the sandbar is what we are on now. The water must have gone down considerably," Elwin said. "Still, stranger things have happened."

"Well, I suppose the real question is how we are going to get across," Sarah said. "It extends as far as we can see to the left and right, and it appears to be at least a half mile across."

"Our barge is destroyed," Elwin said. "We could make a new one, but it would take all day."

"Maybe we could try to swim, you know, if we took our time and rested a lot," Lily said. She started to wade out in the water, but it got very deep, very fast. On top of that, some fish brushed up against her leg. Afraid it was a shark, she ran quickly back to land.

"Did you see that?" Lily asked.

The others ran to the edge of the water to look. It was a fish about a foot long swimming upside down.

"Do you know what that is?" Elwin asked.

"A shark?" Lily replied.

"No, it is an upside down fish. It is a fish with special properties. They are really very rare. I wonder what it is doing here."

"I suppose it was caught in the tidal pool when the tide went out," Sarah said.

"No, it is a freshwater fish," Elwin said. "Well, it can survive in brackish water and even ocean water for a time, but it lives in freshwater."

"Perhaps a rainstorm created a river that let out near here when the tide was high, and then it got trapped," Sarah suggested.

"I wonder if we could catch it. Say, I think I have an idea," Elwin said. "Hand me the empty bag our food was in."

Lily pulled out a gallon-sized bag. She handed it to Elwin. He filled it full of water, and then handed it back.

"Hold this while I try to catch it. You must stand very close to me," he said.

Lily followed Elwin out into the water as he came up on the upside down fish, placing his hands slowly onto either side. It was like he was moving in slow motion, slowly, gradually moving his hands closer to the fish so as not to startle it. All of a sudden, he grabbed it tight with both hands and pulled it out of the water. At that moment, his feet lifted up off the ground, and he started to float. His feet seemed to drift upwards toward the sky of their own accord.

"Quick, Lily!" he cried.

Lily came forward, but Elwin was already above her. She held the bag underneath his hands, and he dropped the fish into the bag, which she sealed shut. Then Elwin fell into the water with a splash.

"Oh, I see," Sarah said. "It makes people float when they hold it. But how is that going to help us? If we grab the fish, we would just keep floating up into the sky forever, unless we could control where we float to."

"You are correct. You would just keep floating up, but I have a solution for that," Elwin said.

Elwin started to dig through his pack until he found a large coil of rope, which at their size was more like a spool of thread. Then he walked up and down the beach for a few minutes until he found what he was looking for – a large piece of driftwood sticking up out of the water. To them, it appeared as an enormous tree extending a hundred yards into the water. They walked out onto the piece of wood, which appeared to them to be a dozen yards wide. By the time they walked to where the knotted end of the wood stuck ten feet out of the water, they had to be a quarter of the way across the tidal pool.

Elwin tied the rope to the end of the driftwood, and then explained, "Tie the rope to your waist and then grab the fish, keeping the bag with you. Once you reach the end of the rope, the wind should carry you toward the shore. Make sure you don't go over the land. When you are near the far side, put the fish back in the bag, and then you will fall into the water. Once you drop in the water, tie the end of the rope to the bag, and we can drag it back."

It seemed a complicated method to get across, but they realized they would not be able to swim without a good rest in the middle, and there was no boat. It was the quickest way.

Sarah agreed to go first. She tied the rope to her, packed up her bag, took the fish out, and quickly sealed its bag and put it into her pack. By this time, she was already starting to float feet first toward the sky. The fish was slimy, but it did not wiggle much once she had it in her hands, perhaps because it was afraid of falling into the water. She continued to float up, up, up. She looked at her feet and saw nothing but sky. She looked down and saw Lily and Elwin standing on the driftwood. They already seemed forty or fifty feet below her. She looked again a few minutes later, and they were now a hundred feet or more below her. She could see the shore for some ways, but it took her a moment to get used to looking at everything upside down. She could see the campfire where they ate their dinner. From this height, the tidal pool seemed only a few feet wide. Across the pool, she could see the castle, its highest tower standing even higher than she was.

Suddenly, Sarah jerked to a stop. She looked at the rope and saw it was fully extended. She was somewhere out over the middle of the tidal pool. She sat still for a moment, and sure enough, a wind was blowing from the ocean behind her. The wind caught her clothes, and she felt herself being pushed toward the far shore. After a few minutes, she looked down and saw that directly below her was land. She had drifted too far. She waited another few minutes, hoping she would drift back, but the wind never died down. It would take all day at this rate. Then she had an idea. Placing the fish under one arm, she grabbed the rope with one hand and pulled it, then grabbed it with the other hand. She continued to reel herself in until she was over the water once more. She almost dropped the fish once, and she tied a loop of the rope around it just in case. But she worked carefully and slowly until she was out deep enough in the water she could risk a fall from her height. Then she put the fish back into the bag and sealed it.

Even as she did so, Sarah fell down, down, down, landing in the water. It was actually very scary, and she closed her eyes so as not to see the fall. She hit the water and opened her eyes when she had reached the surface. She swam toward the castle until she was able to touch the bottom with her feet. Then she tied the rope to the bag as instructed, and waved at Elwin and Lily to let them know it was ready.

Elwin and Lily pulled the bag over, and Sarah waded onto the shore. It seemed like they fiddled around with everything for some time, for it was several minutes before she saw something rising up. She looked closely – it was both Elwin and Lily. Evidently, they thought it best for both to go at the same time, so they had tied themselves together. A few minutes later, they had reached the end of the rope and started to float across the tidal pool. Then they dropped into the water. A few minutes later, they swam to shore and joined Sarah there.

"Did you let the fish go?" Sarah asked.

"No," Lily said, looking down into her backpack. "I thought it might come in handy."

"Well, here we are at last," Elwin said.

They all looked up at the sandcastle towering before them.

# 19

# Inside the Sandcastle

The sandcastle loomed in front of Sarah, Lily, and Elwin. Even though it was still what seemed miles away, it appeared to touch the clouds before them, blocking a quarter of the sky from view. It was as if a skyscraper of sand had been dropped before them. Even through the girls had built the castle, it seemed ominous and evil, filling them with a deep sense of dread.

The castle was, from the outside, very similar in design to what the girls had built. The keep itself was on a large mound raised a hundred feet. It had numerous towers and balconies up to a hundred and fifty or two hundred feet tall, but the central tower was most impressive. It climbed what was at their height several hundred feet. At their normal height, it was well over three feet, coming up to Lily's chest. Surrounding the keep was an impenetrable wall with but two gates. One, the main gate, was on the opposite side of the castle from them. The other was a smaller gatehouse with a sheltered staircase leading down to a boathouse below. Surrounding the wall was a moat. It was, actually, more than a moat, being a large canyon fed by a river from the sea behind them that flooded each time the tide rose, but it was deep enough that there was standing water. On the outside of the moat were more walls and buildings, and then the town, with several hundred outbuildings and huts. These were protected by an outer wall with smaller towers that encircled the whole, other than the canyon and the moat.

The town wall was still some half a mile in front of Elwin and the girls. Between them and the castle were hundreds of sand dunes, like a desert. The only thing that kept it from becoming like the Sahara was the constant sea wind, which, full of moisture from the crashing waves behind them, kept the sand slightly moist. It felt more like beach sand and not desert sand, and for the first few hundred yards it was clumpy and wet from the sea.

After they stood staring at the obstacles they faced, Elwin said, "Well, I suppose we must start walking. The way I figure it, Barracuda has already made it to Triton with his trident. If that is the case, it is only a matter of hours before he starts to make his move on the Sand Wizard."

The girls looked up at the sky. It was still sunny, but there were some clouds gathering far off over the ocean. It was now afternoon.

"Perhaps it would be faster to take the river down the moat to the boathouse," Lily said.

"Where would we get the boat when we did not have one to cross the tidal pool?" Sarah asked.

"Good point," Lily replied.

"Best to leg it, then," Elwin said.

The three of them set off across the sand dunes in the direction of the castle. It was hot work. The temperature was very warm, and they tired quickly. Elwin took the lead with his long stride, followed by Sarah, who liked to be in the front. Lily came up the rear, but eventually she passed Sarah. Surprisingly, Lily seemed to fare better after a while. Her legs had grown long over the past year, and she had worked hard at school at getting in shape because she liked her P.E. teacher. They walked up and down the hills of sand. Once or twice they ran into deep gorges leaving large drops – cliffs of sand – that they could not descend, and they had to work their way around a different direction. Still, they continued on, up and down the sand dunes.

After about two hours, they came to the outer wall of the town. Lily was amazed that, instead of the roughly sculpted sand castle of loose sand they had made, the walls appeared sharp and solid, as though made of stone. She placed her hand on the wall. It was still sandy, but it did not give way as the loose sand should have. It was more like a sandy stone. Further, Lily noticed details that she and Sarah had not designed. The battlements were also sharply sculpted, and the roofs of the towers were now solid and appeared to be supported by timbers. Although there were sometimes twigs in the sand they had used, as with any beach sand, they had not purposely placed these as supports. Then there were the windows. The girls usually just poked holes with their fingers. Now, there were windows with shutters. It must be the fairy magic, Lily thought. The one thing that surprised her was that there were no people – no fairies or gnomes or brownies or anything. It was like the whole town was abandoned.

"Well, how are we going to get past the walls?" Sarah asked.

"Maybe one of the gates we made will still be open," Lily replied.

"There," Elwin pointed some distance down the wall. "It looks like a little hole from here, but it must be huge to be visible at this distance."

They walked along the wall until they came to a spot where the outer wall had collapsed. The sand behind was smooth and dark, as though a wave had come up to this spot at some point and hit against the wall. It must have eroded the bottom, making the wall collapse. Still, they saw no one manning the nearest towers.

"Well, this is where we can get in, but before we do, let's take a little break and talk strategy," Elwin said.

Sarah, Lily, and Elwin had been walking so long and had been so hot, none of them had noticed until that moment how hungry they were. So they found a shady spot at the base of the wall underneath one of the towers. They sat down and pulled out the last of the snack food that Lily and Sarah had brought from the elves. While not filling, it would satisfy them at least until evening. After that, they were not sure what they needed to do. Perhaps the mission would be over by then, or perhaps they would find some other food. Either way, they could not stop now to catch fish or hunt.

"Now, we are getting ready to enter the castle," Elwin said. "You designed it, correct? Tell me about it."

"We designed it, but a lot seems to have changed, not so much to the layout as to the details. The way we built it, the town wall runs around in a large perimeter about six feet or so," Sarah said. "At our height, that would be about a mile or possibly two in diameter. Within this wall is the town, which we made of mostly random square structures. The main gate is on the other side, but it is guarded by two sets of gates, one at the bridge over the moat and one in the inner wall. There is also a door in the keep."

"That sounds imposing," Elwin said. "Is there another way?"

"There is the gate by the boathouse," Lily said. "It has only a single gate and a door, but you would have to get past the wall surrounding the ravine leading down to the sea and then climb down to the stairs."

"Based on what we saw, that would also be pretty difficult to get to," Elwin said. "What would you recommend?"

"We designed the front gates to be open most of the time, and the gate into the keep is also open," Sarah said. "The door by the boathouse we designed to be closed. Who can say if it is unlocked or if we can break it down?"

"My vote would be to work our way around to the front gate to see if it is open," Elwin said. "It seems a little dumb to just walk in the front door, but maybe he watches it less because it is so secure compared to the backdoor, which is the logical approach from the sea. The worst that could happen if the gates are locked is we would have to come back to the door and see if we can break it open."

They all agreed to try this approach.

"What about the interior of the castle?" Elwin asked.

"I'm not sure what that will be like," Sarah said. "We built it as a solid sand block. Other than the gates, towers, and balconies, we did not try to make interior walls."

"The only exception is the courtyard. On one side was a courtyard open to the air," Lily added.

"Well, I suppose we will have to explore it carefully," Elwin said. "It may take some additional time to figure out where everything is. We will especially need to find where he is keeping prisoners, since one of our tasks is to set them free. As for the courtyard, we should use it as a rally point. If you get lost or if you get cornered, get to that courtyard. From there, we can call on the help of the birds or the sprites to help us get away.

"One more word of warning," Elwin added. "The wizard could appear at any time. He is sure to be watching. We must now move with more stealth and be wary. Sarah, I suggest you use your cloak. It may not be able to hide all of us, but it is a lot easier to spot three people than two or one. Everyone ready? Let's go."

Sarah, Lily, and Elwin returned to the hole in the wall and easily climbed over the rubble and into the town. By this time, it was now long after noon, and the shadows were starting to grow. They moved inside the wall and behind the nearest building, staying in the shadows as much as possible. It appeared to be some kind of shed. Once again, Sarah and Lily were amazed that the little lump of sand they had called a house actually turned out to be so detailed and realistic when they were close up to it. They passed a series of houses, all small one-room numbers with similar doorways and no windows. In one or two, they saw furniture. It appeared as though someone had lived there not too long ago. Behind some of the houses were sheds or barns, all much more realistic than the buildings they had made, but there were no people.

"The place is deserted," Sarah started to say, but the words stuck in her throat. It seemed a mistake to make any noise at all because of the echoes they made, so they all kept to silence. Sarah then put on her cloak.

The three of them continued down one street that went for many hundreds of yards, ducking from one shadow to another, making sure to keep the buildings on their right between them and the castle to hide them as much as possible. Finally, they could see ahead of them the northern city wall with its towers fully intact. When they came to the next intersection, they turned to the east, keeping the castle – now to their right – on the other side of the houses and sprinting ahead down to each building. At last, they came to a place where there were no new buildings. A wide avenue turned to the south, and there, past the last house on the lane, were the twin towers of the castle gatehouse. As Sarah had said, the gates were open.

Elwin and the girls watched the gate for some time, expecting some creature or another to be guarding the entrance to the castle, but they saw no one. After another few minutes had expired, Elwin whispered, "I do not see anyone. I think we can try to get through. But be wary. If he does not have guards, there is sure to be a trap of some kind."

Sarah, Lily, and Elwin crept along, keeping to the edge of the road until they reached the base of the towers at the front of the bridge. As an elf, Elwin could move almost completely without sound; Sarah and Lily were not so talented, and he had to shush them several times, for it was so silent you could hear a pin drop.

Elwin sidled over to the gate and peered within. He could still see no one moving within, nor did he hear even the slightest motion. He saw out the other side of the gate that the bridge across the moat was also empty. He waved the girls to him. "Run," he whispered to them, and then set out sprinting across the bridge. Sarah and Lily arrived right behind him when he hit the wall at the base of the second set of towers on the far side of the bridge. Once again, he peered within, but saw no one and nothing. He waved to them again, and they joined him as he slipped inside, blending in with the shadows as he went.

The entrance hall that stood before them was dark and empty, as lifeless as the rest of the town. It stretched the length of the inside of the inner gate, about a hundred feet. The ceiling was high, possibly to the roof of the keep. They could not see it because of the darkness, but Sarah thought there was a balcony above them. The wall about twenty feet in front of them was flat other than a wooden double door directly ahead of them.

Elwin and the girls tiptoed quietly to the door, which was reinforced with iron. It was very heavy and creaked when Elwin pulled on the handle. As a result, he only cracked it open far enough for them to slip through. Once they did, he pulled it closed even slower to avoid creaking. Then they turned to see where they were.

Elwin expected to see a great hall, with a fireplace, dais, throne, and tables, as one might expect in a castle. It was a great hall, but instead of a floor, there were dozens of little walls, about ten feet high and five feet wide leading in different directions, almost like paths. In between were a series of drops or holes into who could say what kind of pit, for there was no floor visible other than the little walls. He and the girls heard the distant sound of water lapping against a wall coming from the pits, so they guessed that it bottomed out into ocean water somewhere below. They looked at the walls and could see from their vantage that several of them dead-ended or led in the wrong direction while others wound around this way and that. It was a maze. Stairs from the door they entered led down into one side of the maze. On the other end, stairs led out of the maze to another door.

"Oh, this is going to take forever," Sarah said. "How can we make it through in enough time if the storm is coming?"

"I guess we just need to get started and hope we make the right turns," Lily said.

"No, there is another way," said Elwin. "Now is the time for the upside-down fish again. All we need to do is hold it, and we will float upside-down. That way, we can just walk across the ceiling above the maze and head straight for the door on the other side."

"Great idea," Sarah said.

Lily pulled out the fish they had caught in the tidal pool, and they all grabbed it together. When they did, they quite suddenly floated up to the ceiling. After making a few tests, they found as long as they touched each other, the magic of the fish worked on all of them. Immediately, they were faced with several problems they had not thought of before. To begin with, the ceiling was vaulted and made of smooth pieces of sandstone with pine timber at the joints. Large chains hung down holding chandeliers. When they floated up, they landed on the edge of the hall, but because of how slippery the ceiling was, they started to slide towards the center where the roof was higher. At first, they tried to resist sliding, but decided it would be easier to just go with the flow.

Once they were on the ceiling, they walked along the center of the vault, carefully walking above and around the various obstacles – the chandeliers, the wide support beams, the buttresses that held up the sides of the hall. Above them (or below depending on your perspective), they passed over the maze. Sarah stopped to look. She could make out the right path, but then she saw it dead end. So she followed another path with her eyes, and it turned several times only to end by running back into itself. She was getting really interested when Elwin poked her to keep moving.

Walking on the ceiling was actually very easy once you got used to the perspective. For the first few minutes, Elwin and the girls felt like they were on their heads and everything was wrong. Once they adjusted, however, they actually started to look at the ceiling like it was the floor and the floor like it was the ceiling. It was like they were in a strange new world.

When the three of them got to the other end of the hall, they realized another problem with their idea. Once they let go of the fish, they would fall down on their heads. They needed to make it into a room that had a shorter ceiling, or they might get hurt. In the room with the vaulted ceiling, they were too far from the door below them to reach it.

It was Lily who figured out how to get down. Noticing that their shoes were too slick on the ceiling, she decided to take hers off. After she carefully stripped down to her bare feet while still touching the fish, she saw that she could get more traction and could actually walk up (or down) the ceiling to the edge of the room. From there, she could walk along a beam that ran the length of the room until she was right over the door. Quickly, Sarah and Elwin followed Lily's lead and were standing above the door.

"How do we get down, though?" Elwin asked. "We might risk letting go of the fish and dropping down, although I would hate to hit those stairs the wrong way."

"I think it would be better to stay on the ceiling a little longer," Sarah said. "If I stand on your shoulders, I think I can reach the top of the door."

So Sarah climbed up onto Elwin's shoulders.

"I can't quite reach," she said. "Lily, come get on my shoulders."

Lily climbed up on Sarah's shoulders and was able to grab the door frame.

"Hold on," Elwin whispered. "I will climb up, or down, or whatever."

Elwin handed Sarah the fish, and she held onto Lily. Then he climbed down and, turning up right, dropped onto the floor in front of the door. Sarah came next, and Elwin helped catch her. Finally came Lily, who flipped over and landed on her feet like a cat. They had made it past the maze.

Elwin opened the door, and the three of them went through it into the next room. Another staircase went down into a set of hallways and rooms. From above, it looked like many bedrooms, each with its own door.

"Perhaps that is where they are keeping the prisoners," Sarah suggested.

The girls followed by Elwin ran down the stairs to the first door on their right. They opened it, and it was empty. There was no furniture or anything else. They went to the next door, and it was the same. After they searched four or five rooms, they discovered that they were all empty.

"This is nothing but a distraction," Elwin said.

Suddenly, as the three of them were speaking, a strong wind started blowing across the room. It appeared to be coming from the walls and not up the hallway as one might expect. They almost lost their footing, the wind was so strong, and the girls only were able to stay upright by imitating Elwin and placing one foot behind them. The sand started flying off the walls and into their eyes. Sarah and Lily placed their hands in front of their eyes. It was blinding them. They felt just as they did when the storm started on the beach, with little pellets of sand striking them and rubbing their skin raw. They threw themselves to the ground.

"Look," Elwin said.

The girls squinted, trying to keep the sand out of their eyes. As the wind continued, they saw that the walls were disappearing to each side of them as the wind knocked them down. At the same time, the sand was collecting in a line across the hallway, forming a new wall in front of them. At first, it was just a line of sand, as though it was collecting against an invisible wall, but it soon began to take a square shape and stacked higher and higher. The wind continued to blow for a few more minutes and suddenly quit. When they opened their eyes, the sand drifting across the floor was gone. Everything was neat and orderly, but instead of a hallway with several rooms, a wall blocked their way with doors on either side.

"It must be some kind of trick of the wizard's," Elwin said as the girls got to their feet.

Elwin opened the door to their left. It was a long chamber with another door on the far side. They crossed and opened it into another chamber, this time with a door on the right. They entered the door, and there was another chamber with doors ahead and on the left.

"It's another maze," Lily said, looking up. "Only this time, we can't go around it."

The walls of the rooms went up to a ceiling about ten feet over their heads. If there was space above them, it was beyond the ceiling of sand.

Sarah, Lily, and Elwin went through the door ahead, and inside was another chamber with doors to the left and right. They went left and came into a room with no doors. It was a dead end. So they went back and took the door to the right. They went through one room after another until they came to another empty room.

"We have gone about the same distance that we went to the left from the hallway," Elwin said. "The door to the other staircase should be right here."

"Maybe it is hidden," Sarah said.

Elwin and the girls searched the wall for some kind of hidden door or trap door in the floor or ceiling. They backed up a few rooms to see if they had missed some turn that might take them to the stairs, but they found nothing.

"I am telling you, the door should be right here," Elwin said.

"Well, the walls are only sand. Maybe we can make a door," Lily said.

"Good idea," Elwin said, drawing his sword. The girls also pulled out their elven knives and started to dig through the wall.

The three of them were just starting to make progress with their knives when the wind started to blow again. It pushed them back from the wall. The sand was stripping from the walls beside them and forming a wall in front of them. Elwin tried to stop it, but the wind knocked him down. The sand continued to fly from different directions. Sarah backed away from the wall but found herself against a wall forming behind her. She looked to the left and right, and walls were forming all around them.

"We are being walled in!" Sarah shouted.

"We must get out!" Elwin shouted back.

Suddenly they heard a maniacal laugh echoing through the wind. It was the Sand Wizard.

"This way," Elwin said and jumped over the wall behind them.

The wall was now too high for the girls to step over, so they ran and dove over the top, landing on the floor beyond with a tuck and roll. The wind was still whipping sand around them. They pushed their way through the sandstorm until they came to a door. It did not appear to be moving with the walls as with the other doors.

"It's an exterior door," Elwin shouted.

"The courtyard," Lily and Sarah said together.

Sarah, Lily, and Elwin pushed through the driving wind and sand whipping around them until they made it to the wall. They opened the door, and saw an open space with no sand or wind. They looked up and saw the sky and another wall of the sandcastle across the way. They stepped out into the courtyard, for that is indeed where they were. They had escaped from the chamber of moving sand.

# 20

# The Sand Man Cometh

It seemed a little cooler out in the courtyard than it did inside the sandcastle. Sarah, Lily, and Elwin looked up at the sky again. It also seemed a little darker and overcast than it had before they had gone into the castle. There were black storm clouds gathering ominously far overhead. The wind had picked up a little, but it was moist and refreshing, not full of sand. The girls breathed deeply. They could not help but feel that they had had a narrow escape and were glad to be out in the open again.

Suddenly, they heard the same voice laughing maniacally far overhead. They looked up and saw a figure standing on a balcony above them. It was Somnambulus, though they could not see him distinctly and did not know what he looked like. But they could tell it was a tall figure with blond hair the color of sand streaked with grey, and a yellow and tan robe. Next to him stood another smaller figure, a woman, with black hair and a similarly colored robe. It was the Sand Witch.

"You think you have escaped me because you are outside?" Somnambulus shouted. "But there is as much sand here as there is below. Get them my soldiers!"

As the wizard shouted, Sarah, Lily, and Elwin could see the walls of the sandcastle trembling, and dust seemed to fall off of the walls as a shape moved out into the open. It appeared as a man with very rough features, only the man was made entirely of sand. The creature held a shield and a spear of some kind, all made of sand. It stepped toward the girls, dropping dust and sand as it moved. A second stepped out of another part of the wall, then a third. Within a minute, there were a half dozen of the soldiers.

Elwin pulled out his sword, and Sarah and Lily their daggers. Elwin swung at the nearest of the sand people. His sword cut through its arm, which fell to the ground like a piece of wet sand. Yet before he could strike again, dust flew from the creature's outer body and formed another arm and shield. The sand man appeared a little smaller, but it was whole again. Sarah's and Lily's blows had similar effect. Meanwhile, the sand people struck out with their spears. One of them caught the hem of Sarah's cloak, which she had thrown back behind her head when they had entered the castle. The spear, although made of sand, had a point that was as sharp as a piece of quartz, as though it was made of a single large grain of sand. It stuck fast into the sand at their feet, and the only way she could get out was to duck out of the cloak, leaving it pinned to the ground.

The sand people continued to surround them, when Elwin put away his sword.

"What are you doing?" Lily shouted.

"The swords do no good," Elwin said, bending down and picking up a piece of driftwood. "Let's try a mace."

Elwin broke off a limb until only a large club remained, fat at the top with a long, thin handle, like a baseball bat. He wound up at the nearest sand man and swung. The club struck it full on the shoulders, shattering its head into a million particles of sand as he knocked it off his shoulders. Elwin followed up with a kick against its chest, and it fell over, breaking into globs of sand. He had figured out how to defeat them, but there were still five left to threaten them, and another six stepped out of the walls.

"We can defeat them, but not like this, not together as they face us," Elwin said. "There is only one thing we can do. We must separate. That will give you the opportunity to search for the prisoners, while drawing off the sand people. Then we can attack them when we can."

"But we will get lost," Sarah said.

"You must trust you will find your way. If you can, meet back here or at the gate. Once you get to one of those places, you can make it out," Elwin said.

The three of them agreed and ran in different directions – Sarah up the stairs behind them, Lily through the door back into the hall from which they came, and Elwin across the courtyard to an exterior tower. The sand people, confused by seeing them running in different directions, bumped into each other as they tried to follow, with the result that Lily got through the door and Sarah got up the stairs before the sand people knew what was happening. The only one who was still out in the open was Elwin, so most of the sand people took off after him.

Elwin made it across the courtyard to the tower door and turned to face the first of the sand men who had followed him. He struck one with a club and then another, knocking their heads off, then he swung at their legs, knocking them down as they dematerialized. Still, more came behind him. He opened the door rapidly and struck another full in the chest with it as it swung out on its hinges. The creature staggered back, its shield crumbling to dust in front of it, and another club blow was all that it took to dissolve it. Elwin then closed the door behind him. He had to wait only seconds when one of the sand people started to open the door. He kicked it hard, striking it with his full force, and the creature instantly shattered. He waited another few seconds, and another of the mindless creatures pulled on the door. A second time, he kicked the door causing an instant explosion of sand. He waited another few seconds, but none pulled at the door. He instantly bounded up a spiral staircase behind him.

Elwin passed two doors on one level, but one of them was being opened by one of the sand people, so he continued up the stairs to reach a trapdoor in the roof. Pushing it open, he came through and realized that he was trapped. Across the courtyard on a balcony above him, Elwin could see the Sand Wizard, now standing alone with his arm extended and his eyes closed as though in deep concentration controlling the creatures. On every side of Elwin, however, were the battlements and a sharp drop of twenty feet or more to the parapet on the top of the walls.

After a few seconds, one of the sand people kicked open the trapdoor, climbing onto the top of the tower. Elwin made use of his club to destroy it quickly. By the time he did, two more were on the tower roof. He attacked them, shattering a shield and a spear before he knocked one off the tower and destroyed the other. When he turned back, there were half a dozen, with more waiting for room to climb up. Elwin set to work quickly destroying one after another, knocking them off the tower, destroying their legs so they fell on the ground and into dust, or crushing their heads and bodies.

Elwin continued to fight as another came up through the hole. He knew that he was tiring and would soon lack the energy to fight back. He had to do something to change the situation, but what? Perhaps if he could get rid of the Sand Wizard, the creatures would not be able to challenge him.

Acting quickly, Elwin knocked the next two creatures off the roof with one blocking maneuver, and then he ran to the trapdoor and flipped it onto the legs of another, killing it. Kneeling on the top of the trapdoor, he pulled out his bow and notched an arrow, taking careful aim for the Sand Wizard. He shot, but the arrow missed and instead stuck into the door behind the wizard. Elwin shot again, and the wizard threw up a dust screen which seemed to block the arrow. A third arrow and a fourth were enough to convince the wizard to flee through the door. Elwin watched for his return, but the wizard was gone.

The elf opened the door, and another sand man was climbing up, which he smashed with the trapdoor again. This time, however, the wooden trapdoor broke off the hinges. Elwin grabbed the trapdoor, and, using it like a shield pushed through the trapdoor, knocking a sand man in front of him off the stairs and into the stairwell below. Elwin got on his hands and knees on the trapdoor and started sliding down the staircase like he was on a sled. As he did, he crushed the legs of a half dozen sand people, which plummeted to their deaths as they fell into the stairwell.

When Elwin got back down to the bottom of the stairs, there were no more sand people left. He looked around. All he saw was a pile of sand at the bottom of the stairwell. With the Sand Wizard gone, the creatures were not getting up but simply turned into sand again. Elwin ran out into the courtyard, but there were no more sand people, nor were any forming from the sand walls. He quickly entered the nearest door back into the sandcastle to look for Lily and Sarah.

Meanwhile, Lily had run back into the hall of moving sand. Surprisingly there were no walls at all. It seemed to her that now the Sand Wizard no longer was focused on them all of the walls had dropped into nothingness, leaving a smooth sand floor up to the stairs leading out of the hall. Lily ran across, half expecting a wall to pop up at any moment, but she made it to the stairs and opened the door. Inside was another broad hall, similar in size and shape to the entrance hall. That meant that somewhere above her was a balcony and across the way were some towers and probably stairs as well. It also meant the door to the boat house was about one level down. If only she could get there, she could open it so they would have a way to escape.

Lily started to close the door behind her with a creak, when she saw one of the sand people in the hall she had just left. It had evidently just come in through the door leading to the courtyard. She kept the door cracked, so she could watch the creature as it searched the room, first by going back to the door into the maze room to check if she was there, and then by heading toward the stair and door into the rear hall, where she was.

As there was no way to escape the sand man before it caught up with her, Lily had to get rid of it. Her mind raced and remembered the rope. Perhaps she could rig a trap. She saw two heavy stone benches on either side of the door, and quickly strung the rope between them at about ankle level. Then she started to head toward the tower. The sand man opened the cracked door and ran through just as Lily was at one of the tower doors. It tripped on the rope and landed on the smooth hard floor, breaking into a million grains of sand. Lily made it to the tower and shut the door behind her.

A spiral staircase led up and down into the darkness. Thinking that she could find the back gate, Lily went down. Coming to the base of the tower, she found a door that opened up into another large hall. Sure enough, in the center of the back wall, there was a large double door, with a wooden brace locking it shut. She pulled up on the heavy beam and threw it onto the floor. She pulled on the door handle. It was enormously heavy, but she was able to open it a crack and could see the stairway leading down to the boat house and the canyon filled with water.

Lily turned back to the darkness of the castle. In front of her, mostly obscured by the darkness, was another door directly across the hall. She walked across the way and opened the door. Inside was another long hallway with rooms on either side. This time, however, the walls stayed put as she walked inside. Then she saw that there were metal bars across each room. It was the dungeon!

Lily ran inside, and in the dim light, she could just make out that each cell contained some creature. The first contained some gnomes with their pointed hats. The second contained fairies, their wings clipped. The third contained a giant crab. The fourth contained a large metal and glass water tank holding two mermaids. She tried to shake the bars but something prevented her from even approaching.

"Hey! I've come to rescue you," Lily shouted.

But none of them moved. She looked at each carefully, but they all seemed asleep.

"Triton said something about the Sand Wizard's ability to put creatures to sleep," Lily said to herself. "It has to be his magic."

Lily tried to open the gates, but they were all locked. She looked for keys, but could not find any. She tried to bend the bars with a piece of wood, but they were too strong.

"Still, at least I know where they are, and that they are near a way out. I will find the others and tell them," she said.

Lily ran up the stairs, peeking carefully around corners to make sure that the sand people were not waiting for her. All she had to do was locate the others and take them down to the dungeon to help her release the prisoners. Afraid she could not find her way back, she carved little arrows into the walls of the tower and next to each door through which she came. She would find her way back and release them all.

While Elwin fought the sand people and Lily found the prisoners, Sarah had run up the stairs with two sand men on her heels. The first she was able to dispose of easily enough when at the head of the stairs she dropped down and kicked its legs from under it. The thing crashed backwards, narrowly missing the second one, only to strike the stairs about halfway down and break into pieces. As the thing tumbled, it broke into additional pieces until nothing but a cloud of dust was left at the foot of the stairs. This actually helped her escape, since the other sand men in the courtyard could not see past the cloud and turned to chase Elwin, who quickly reached the door of a tower across the way.

By the time Sarah regained her feet, the other sand man was at the top of the stairs and trying to grab her. She took off running across a balcony to an interior door. She opened it and closed it, then moved to a second door leading into a bedroom with furniture, which she closed behind her. She looked around, but there was no other way out of the room, not even a window.

If the sand man figured out Sarah came that way, she would be trapped. The door opened out, so she could not kick it into the sand man. Instead, she would have to find another way to get rid of it. She looked around and saw a chest at the foot of the bed. Perhaps she could hide there, she thought, but decided it was the first place most people would look. Then she saw a screen in a corner of the room.

Sarah was just about to look around the screen when the doorknob started to turn, and she ducked behind it. She crouched down and looked out from behind the screen every few seconds to see what the sand man did as it stepped into the room. First, it looked at the corner of the room, and then it looked under the bed. Seeing the chest, the thing positioned itself with its back to Sarah. She saw it open the chest and took a chance. She charged the sand man, hitting it square in the back with her shoulder. It was a little like hitting rock. Still, she managed to knock it over and into the chest. Then she promptly slammed the lid on top of it. Waiting a few seconds, she opened the lid. All that was left was a boxful of sand.

Sarah ran out of that bedroom and through two more rooms until she was standing in a hallway. Suddenly, the Sand Wizard walked around a corner. He did not seem as surprised to see her as she was of him. He started to walk toward her. Sarah ran in the opposite direction down the hallway. She turned a corner and ran down a set of stairs and partway across a large chamber below, when a cloud of sand appeared on the opposite side of the room. The sand swirled in a circle like a dust devil for several seconds when the Sand Wizard started to appear in the midst of the cloud. She could just make out his head and torso, like some genie appearing in smoke from a bottle.

In seconds, the wizard would be fully materialized, so Sarah turned to run. She opened a door behind her and ran into another large room, closing the door quickly to hide her path. She took a few steps across the room. Again, the cloud of sand started to form as the wizard appeared before her. This time, however, Sarah picked up a small stool and threw it into the swirling dust, hoping to prevent the wizard from taking human form. Then she shut the door as she backed out of the room and sprinted down another hallway. The cloud of dust seemed to follow her down the hall, like a little tornado. As it passed her, she could make out the face of the wizard in the sand laughing at her.

Sarah immediately cut right into another room, ran across it to a door, and was through it before the cloud of sand could change directions. Bearing in mind that he knew the castle well and could guess the most logical direction she would go, she tried to make her movements random by cutting left or right, through doors, upstairs, and around corners. In the end, she herself was lost. She did not know what floor she was on or exactly what part of the castle she was in.

Sarah ran up another set of stairs and turned down a hallway with a door at the end. She had gone maybe halfway down the corridor in that direction when the door opened and a woman stepped in from the balcony. It was the Sand Witch. Sarah paused a second, but the woman did not seem to react, so she continued to run, hoping she could get past the witch and maybe down the balcony.

The woman, seeing Sarah run toward her, raised her hands, palms upward. A wind picked up in the tunnel, blowing the woman's jet black hair into the air. Sand started to kick up from the floor, forming an impenetrable cloud. Sarah could not see or even breathe. She started coughing violently and put up her arm in front of her eyes. She pulled out a handkerchief to breathe through, and threw herself on the ground, hoping to find a space where the air was clear.

When the dust finally settled and she looked up, she could see the bare feet of the woman standing only a few feet from her. She looked behind her, and there were the sandaled feet and yellow robe of the wizard. They were on either side of her, looking down at her. She was trapped!

# 21

# The Tower

Lily climbed the stairs from the dungeon and arrived outside the room of moving sand. She looked around for Sarah or Elwin, but, seeing no one, she made her way back outside to the courtyard. Afraid that more of the sand men would come after her, she stood by the exterior door and peeped out from time to time. She did not see anyone there either. After waiting some minutes and not seeing any sand men or other threats, Lily decided to go out into the courtyard to search for her sister. She put her hood over her head and stepped out into the day. Still, she did not move more than a few inches beyond the door because she was afraid to reveal herself.

Elwin had talked about meeting either in the front hall or the courtyard if they got separated, but no one mentioned how long they should wait for each other. What if Elwin or Sarah had been killed or captured by the sand people? As sad as that was, Lily knew it was a possibility. What if the Sand Wizard was waiting for her to show herself? Just by waiting, she might be ensuring her own capture and the failure of the mission.

Lily looked up at the clouds moving overhead. The sky was now dark and overcast. A heavy wind was blowing from the sea, whipping up the sand. She could smell the salt air. She knew that the storm was coming soon. Soon she would run out of time. They would all be drowned when the waves crashed down on the castle, as Lily knew would eventually happen. She had to do something, anything, to try to find out what had happened to Sarah and Elwin.

Lily tried to see the balcony above her, but it was difficult for her to see more than the bottom of it from her position below. She saw no one moving and no one standing on the balcony and decided that it might be safe. Plucking up some courage, Lily stepped out to move toward the stairs that she had seen Sarah start to climb. She kept to the base of the wall and then started to climb up. Perhaps she would find Sarah if she went this way.

"Lily," she heard a voice say. Looking up, Lily saw Elwin standing above her on the landing and the top of the stairs.

"Thank goodness you are all right. Have you seen Sarah?" Elwin asked.

"Not since we parted," Lily replied.

"We must find her, and fast. The storm is about to break, and I fear once it does we will have little time to search," Elwin responded.

"The last time I saw her, she went this way," Lily said, pointing toward the door at the top of the stairs leading into the sandcastle.

"That is not good," Elwin said. "I saw the Sand Wizard go in that door over there into the same part of the castle. Maybe they did not meet, but I rather doubt that."

Elwin opened the door, half expecting to see the Wizard standing there in the hallway, but there was only an empty corridor. He and Lily went down the hall until they came to a door, opened it slowly, but found only an empty room. They closed the door and went to the next door and empty room. They searched for several minutes, opening every door in the hall and then searching in rooms both down and up several sets of stairs. Lily ran down to the boathouse door, but did not see Sarah. Elwin checked in each of the corner towers. As they did, they said her name as loud as they would dare, louder than a whisper but not quite a yell. They checked the courtyard again, as well as the gates to the castle. They even climbed up on the walls to see if she had gone outside to wait for them, but she was nowhere to be found.

"There is only one other place we have not searched for Sarah," Elwin said. "She must have gone up to the central tower. We have searched most of the rest of the castle."

"Does that mean that she was captured?" Lily asked.

"Not necessarily. She may have gone up of her own freewill so she could search for us from above, though I would not wonder if you were correct, for that is where the Sand Wizard actually lives," Elwin said.

"How do you know that?" Lily asked.

"Because in all of the rooms we have searched, none had a lived-in look or contained the kind of magical equipment you would think a wizard would have. You know, books and wands and stuff. It only makes sense that he lives in the tower, where he can watch comings and goings easier. Of course, there is only one way to know for sure," Elwin answered.

He and Lily went to the top floor of the keep, where a large staircase went up through the center of the ceiling. The spiral staircase turned and turned for as far as they could see above them, getting narrower and narrower as it reached the top.

"Well, this is going to take time," Lily said.

It was like being stuck in the fire escape of the tallest skyscraper, only there was no elevator. Elwin and Lily went round and round, one step at a time. At first, Lily tried to count the steps, but she lost count after a few hundred. They hiked for what seemed like hours, though it was probably only minutes. Lily's legs started to ache from lifting her feet and pushing herself up.

As they climbed, Elwin and Lily passed several windows. They could see the storm clouds gathering. There was lightning far out to sea, and they could hear the thunder. A wind blew through the windows, which was some comfort. At least it was cool in the tower as they climbed and not sweltering hot like in the castle. They continued upwards still. Although they tried to be quiet and did not talk, Lily could not help that her footsteps echoed loudly in the stairwell as they climbed, for being very tired her feet seemed to drop clumsily rather than land lightly on each step, as the elf's did. Perhaps that is what gave away their presence. Regardless, when they reached a landing some halfway up the tower they found it occupied by Somnambulus, waiting for them.

"So the fairy peoples would send an elf and elf friends to do their dirty work," Somnambulus said when he saw them in the dim light. "You would invade my tower with the intent to destroy me?"

Elwin said nothing but set out at a charge up the steps to the platform. It caught Lily off guard, since she was still formulating a plan in her head. She had to sprint to catch up to him and not be left by herself some twenty or thirty yards below them. Elwin drew his sword. Seeing the blade, Lily pulled out the knife the elves gave her. They both seemed to shine as though they were reflecting the lightning of the approaching storm.

Elwin had got no more than a dozen steps forward when the wizard raised his arms with fingers pointing upward. Elwin and Lily heard a rustling. When they looked down, they saw sand streaming through the air. It was pouring through the middle of the tower like sand through an hourglass, only the top and the bottom were reversed. When it reached their height, it wrapped into the form of a snake, weaving around them. The head of the sand snake curved around until it faced Elwin, all the while its folds were tightening round them, first on Lily, then Elwin. Thinking fast, Elwin lifted his arms above the folds, and struck at the head with his sword when it came within range. Two or three well-placed blows shattered the head and cut the folds, allowing him to escape. The wizard then spread out his fingers, and the sand whipped into a storm, blowing around and around about them. Within seconds, the sandstorm blocked the middle of the tower. Lily could barely see, but she could make out the shape of Elwin battling through the sand toward the landing. She could not help but wonder what had happened to her sister.

When Sarah awoke, she found herself lying on a couch in a strange room. On the floor and forming two interior walls were numerous large carpets or tapestries. Curtains of carpets formed all the interior walls and divided them into sections. Only the exterior wall was sandstone, and in it were numerous windows, which lit the room. She guessed she was at the top of the tower, and the windows were between the battlements. Sarah tried to remember how she got there. The sand wizard and witch had trapped her in the corridor. The sand wizard had said something and blown sand into her eyes, and she had lost consciousness.

Waking herself up, Sarah started to look around, peering behind the carpets into the other rooms. In one room, there was a large bed. In another, there was a table with beakers and tubing and a large iron cauldron, as though someone were concocting something. Another was a dining room and kitchen. The room she was in appeared to be a library, only the books seemed very strange. They all had titles about magic or potions. There was a lectern holding a large book. She looked at it and saw that it, too, was a book of spells. There was a spell for summoning creatures from the earth, one for causing sleep, one for controlling the winds, and one to create creatures out of sand. Next to each spell was a picture that seemed to jump out of the page, like other fairy books she had seen. They were more like windows into a real-life scene depicting the effects of the spell, with people that actually moved like a little video or movie. She flipped a few pages, and then turned when she heard someone coming.

It was the Sand Witch. The black-haired woman pulled back the curtain and stepped into the library section of the tower. For a moment, she did not speak, but only looked at Sarah with sad eyes, her dark hair flowing in curls down her shoulders.

"My name is Arenae. I came to see that you were awake with no ill effects from the sleep Somnambulus placed on you, and also to see that you were properly fed," she said.

"Why are you keeping me here? Why did you not kill me like he has so many others?" Sarah asked.

"It is the command of Somnambulus. Anyway, he would only kill those who are hostile to him. Although you and your friends are trying to attack us here, he prefers not to kill you so that he can persuade the others to leave," Arenae said.

"What about all of the mermaids and sea creatures that he has killed trying to control them?" Sarah said. "They were not hostile to him except for swimming where they always swam."

"I do not think this is true," the witch said.

"I have been among them and heard their tales, and I have seen through their magic the attacks upon them. Does he not, even at this moment, have sea creatures imprisoned in this castle that did nothing but go about their lives?" Sarah asked.

Arenae looked thoughtful, and then said, "It matters not. Will you eat something? I will eat with you to assure you that the food is good and not poisoned. Somnambulus does not mean you harm."

"You can believe that if you want," Sarah said. "I suppose I should keep my strength up for whatever torture or trials lie ahead."

Arenae led Sarah into another section of the tower where a table waited on them, already laid out with plates, utensils, and food. It was mostly seafood – crabs, clams, flounder, and other creatures who buried themselves in the sand – with some tropical fruits, such as pineapple, oranges, and mangos. Sarah helped herself to some of the fruit and a little flounder since she was not fond of shellfish. Arenae took some of each of the foods Sarah selected and also a little crab.

After a few minutes of eating, Sarah asked, "So why do you stay with Somnambulus?"

"What do you mean?" Arenae replied.

"I saw your expression. You know that Somnambulus is not as innocent as you claim. He is taking prisoners, including many who have never done anything to him. He is increasingly expanding into the domains of others. He has been talking with the sea hag to get her to attack the merpeople. You know what his plans are. So why do you stay with him?" Sarah asked again.

"I cannot do otherwise. You see, he made me what I am today. I cannot remember a time when I was not with him, and always I have stood by him, even when I do not agree with his actions. I do know that he sometimes exceeds the bounds of nature. Nature has a place and a role for everyone. Like the flowing of the tide, it is self-regulating. The bigger fish hunt the smaller fish, so the smaller fish take to shallow waters where the bigger fish do not stray, and if the bigger fish go into shallow waters, they get trapped and drown. The octopus has its hunting grounds, as do the sharks and rays, but they cannot go many places for nature has set bounds upon them, and they know by instinct where they cannot go. But men are not like that, and as with many men, Somnambulus sometimes oversteps his bounds," Arenae said.

"Then you agree with me that he is not a good man," Sarah said.

"He is not always good, but no man is. He has his designs, and some of what he wants would be good for those he would rule, but, yes, I also do know that some of what he wants would injure others. He wishes only for order, to prevent the randomness that he thinks the merpeople bring to their domain. He would try to create order, though through order he would change the very regimen of those peoples," the woman responded.

"I think his designs are more harmful that you think. Take me, for instance," Sarah said. "I came to this place, not to harm Somnambulus as he has told you, but to release those whom he has imprisoned. I wish to return the crabs and the merpeople to the seas. Yet he has taken me prisoner. He says that he will release me once my friends leave, but they will not leave me, and in any case, were they to leave, what do you think he would do? Would he not also imprison me as he has the others? Or worse, would he kill me because he sees me as a greater threat?"

"I did not know that is why you came," Arenae said. "I have thought of the consequences of your being here, but I thought it was just because you are like the small fish straying into the deeper waters. But now, if you are coming only to release others, like a fisherman letting the dolphin from his nets, I am not sure how to view your actions or his."

"All I want to do is to get back to my friends, release the prisoners, and get out of this sandcastle. I have no desire to even see Somnambulus, let alone try to kill him or stop him from doing whatever he wants. Will you let me at least do that?" Sarah asked.

"I must go and check on Somnambulus to see if he needs help. The stairs down the tower are not open to you. If you escape some other way, there is nothing I can do to stop it," Arenae said. Then she got up from the table and left.

"Now how can I get out of the tower without going down the stairs?" Sarah asked herself out loud.

If she could get in touch with the fairies, Sarah could try to fly down, but she knew they most of them could not come into the castle because of the magic circle. Perhaps she could climb down some other way. She went to one of the windows on the tower and looked down. It was a dizzying height. It was definitely too high to climb from here. Suddenly, she noticed windows every so often circling around the tower, probably following the stairs. Maybe she could get a little lower and climb out the window and back in another window. It was about the only way without killing herself. She searched the tower for some rope, but found none. But there was an enormous bed with sheets. She took the sheets off the bed and tied knots in them to form a rope. Then she quietly followed Arenae down the stairs.

Sarah continued down the stairs until she was right above the platform where she saw Somnambulus moving his arms about as sand whipped this way and that. Arenae was coming up behind him. She dared not go farther down the stairs without revealing herself. She looked around and saw a window. She stuck her head out and saw other windows winding around the tower below her. The problem was how to tie off the sheets, as there was nothing near the window. She looked through her things until she found the elven dagger. Just under the window sill was a large crack. That would have to do, she told herself. She pushed the dagger into the crack until it was stuck fast. Then she tied the sheet rope to the handle and pulled it hard toward the window. It appeared to hold.

Sarah looked out the window again, and her head started to swim, but she knew she must act soon or she would never be able to escape. Saying a quick prayer, she lowered herself out the window holding the rope and walked down the side of the tower. She went down to the bottom of her sheet rope, where she guessed that she was past the platform where the wizard was standing. The problem was that the nearest window was a good ways to her left. She started to swing over. The first couple of tries, she was still far from the window, but she kept swinging until she could see in the window. There was Lily standing behind a cloud of sand looking up.

She swung back and forth again and whispered, "Lily!" She swung back again. By the time she returned, Lily had her head out the window and tried to grab her.

"I can't quite reach you," Lily said.

Sarah swung back again and tried to lean into her swing toward the window. Suddenly, the rope appeared to give way, and she slipped down another two or three feet and then stopped, which must have been due to the dagger slipping from the crack. It was just enough for Sarah to reach the ledge. Lily grabbed her hand just as the rope appeared to give way. She heard the dagger clinking down the wall as the rope fell. Pulling on Lily's hand, she grabbed the window sill and hoisted herself through the window as Lily leaned back until they were both lying on the floor in a pile.

"That was lucky," Sarah said.

As Sarah and Lily sat looking up at the cloud of sand swirling around the tower, Elwin emerged from the dust. "Sarah, where did you come from? Never mind. No time now. You and Lily must go and release the prisoners. I will hold off Somnambulus. Be quick, though. The sea is rising."

Sarah and Lily immediately got up and ran down the stairs.

"But where are the prisoners?" Sarah asked.

"I found them. Follow me," Lily said, and they both charged down the stairs, along the corridor, and to one of the towers that led down to the dungeon.

When they stepped out of the tower, Sarah and Lily noticed that the floor was flooded to a depth of about six inches. The door leading to the boathouse was now open, and the tide was flowing through it. A cold wind was blowing into the hallway. It was almost so strong that it knocked them over. Sarah and Lily fought their way to the dungeon and forced the door open.

"We have to figure out how to get them out," Lily said. "And quick. The water is starting to cover the floor."

"We can use a lever to push the doors off the hinges," Sarah said. "I saw that in a movie."

Sarah and Lily grabbed a bench along one wall to try to lift up one of the cell doors, but when they approached, there was a blue field of energy that prevented them from approaching.

"It's some kind of magical force field," Sarah said.

"Look," Lily said. On the far end of the dungeon was a shelf with a large odd-shaped crystal that glowed blue whenever they approached the cells.

"Grab the crystal and try to open the field long enough for me to get the cell door open," Sarah said, standing by with the bench.

Lily ran down the hall and grabbed the crystal off the shelf. She concentrated on the doors to make them open. She focused on the crystal itself and said in her mind all of the opening words she could remember: open, enter, unlock, undo, release, and remove. Nothing seemed to work. Finally, she got frustrated.

"Stupid thing," she yelled and threw it against the wall. It struck the hard stone and shattered into pieces. The blue light went out, and each of the cell doors flew open.

Sarah and Lily went in and shook each of the creatures awake. The fairies grabbed the gnome and flew out the back door, though not very high from having their wings clipped. The crab ran down the hallway. Other creatures they did not recognize also ran out until all that was left were the mermaids in the tank.

"We will help you," Sarah said to them, then turning to Lily, she added, "Grab the other side of the tank. We will have to carry it closer to the ocean."

"It shouldn't be too far," Lily said as she sloshed through ankle deep water.

The tank was enormously heavy, and it took them many stops before Sarah and Lily had got it to the dungeon door. By this time, the water in the room was knee deep. They took another few steps and finally made it to the boathouse door.

"This is far enough," one of the mermaids said. They pushed themselves out of the tank and into the now waist-deep water. They swam into the entering tide, stopping at the door to wave to Sarah and Lily. Then grabbing the door frame, they pushed themselves through the door into the incoming ocean and were gone.

# 22

# The Storm

Sarah and Lily climbed up the stairs from the dungeon, staying just ahead of the rising tide. Water was coming in the door to the courtyard. Still, they climbed. Once in the keep, they ran down the corridor to the stairs leading up the tower. They paused a moment to peer out a window that looked over the keep to the sea. They saw a giant wave rise over the walls, landing on the roof of the castle. The water drained away to reveal the eroded and ruined castle walls. The form was there, but it was vague and without the detail. It looked like the sandcastle they had originally made.

The girls continued to climb, hoping the height of the tower would protect them. Finally, they came to the spot where Elwin continued to fight off Somnambulus. In front of Elwin was a score of sand people. One by one Elwin struck them down only to have each one replaced by another. It was a battle he knew he could not win. All he had to do, though, was to keep Somnambulus occupied so Sarah and Lily could do their work.

"They are free," Sarah said. "We can go now."

Water was now pouring in the windows from the rain, and wind was whipping through the tower, making it difficult to stand. Suddenly, a wave struck high up on the tower. Water poured down the stairs, making them slippery. The sand people were slipping and falling, some down the depths of the tower. Some were eroding as the wind and water from the windows struck them. Elwin started to back down the stairs slowly. Sarah and Lily were waiting for him below.

"Uh-oh," Lily said.

Sarah and Lily looked down and saw water rising up the tower. Sarah looked out the window and saw that the keep was completely underwater. The flood was rising.

"We must get out, now," Elwin said. "Wait until the water is a little higher, and dive out the window into the water."

The girls continued to watch the water rise, and Sarah looked up. The sand people had dissipated, leaving blobs of wet sand along the stairs. Somnambulus was talking to Arenae. His power seemed to be waning as the water washed away the sand.

"You did this," he was saying to her. "You let the girl escape. I told you to keep her to use as leverage."

"She escaped on her own," Arenae replied. "Besides, she meant no harm to you. She only wished to set free those you had imprisoned."

"You are of no more use to me. With my last effort, I release you," he said.

Suddenly, Arenae turned to sand and blew with the wind out the window. She was nothing but sand to begin with, a creation of his magic and imagination. Now she was gone.

By this point, the water was now just below the nearest window. Lily, Sarah, and Elwin jumped in that order out of the window into the water. They had taken a few strokes from the castle when they saw the tower fall in upon itself as the water knocked it over. Whether Somnambulus was able to get out before that happened, they never did know, but he was never seen or heard from again.

The girls and Elwin looked about them and saw nothing but water in all directions. They could not even see the shore to determine the direction they needed to swim.

"But we are still small," Lily pointed out. "We must get to the potion on the boat."

Sarah, Lily, and Elwin began to swim, while guessing in what direction they had anchored the boat. Wave after giant wave lifted them and then placed them down. They somehow avoided all of the waves that seemed to arch over them, threatening to crash down on them. They found themselves being pulled out into the ocean by a rip tide. In a few minutes, they were out past the largest breakers and saw their boat. A head popped out of the water as they swam up. It was Scallop.

"Hey!" the three tiny people all yelled, trying to get her attention.

With keen eyes, Scallop saw them and swam up to scoop them out of the water and place them on the prow of the boat.

"I have been watching for you all afternoon. I thought you would be showing up right about the time the storm started," Scallop said.

"Quick!" Elwin said. "Get the potion that the elves gave us, so we can return to our normal size."

Scallop searched through several bags on the boat, then pulled out the little potion bottle. She un-stoppered it and held it down where they could reach it, allowing each to take a little drink. Immediately, Sarah's legs popped out like a telescope and into the water. The others followed. Soon, they were all in the water next to the boat.

"Well, we did it!" Lily said.

"I am so glad," Scallop said.

Just then, a huge wave crashed down on them, forcing them all underwater. When the girls came up for a breath, the boat and Elwin were several yards away.

"Quick, swim to them," Sarah said.

Sarah and Lily swam several strokes, but another wave crashed over them. When their heads came up again, Elwin was in the boat, but he was now a dozen yards or more away. Scallop was nowhere to be seen. Another wave came, and they seemed to be drifting even farther apart.

"It must be the magic of the mermaids," Elwin shouted over the torrent. "Return to your lands and be glad for what you have done. We will see each other again someday!"

Elwin waved at them as he continued to drift out into the ocean. They waved back.

"I wish I had had a chance to say goodbye and give him a hug," Lily said.

"Me, too, but sometimes it is better this way," Sarah replied.

The waves continued to pound over their heads until the girls were pushed back onto the beach, where their feet could touch the bottom. They started to wade back onto the beach. They could now see their hotel in front of them, and their father was walking out onto the sand.

"What are you girls doing in the water?" he yelled over the wind. "I thought you were only going to wade a little. Don't you know how dangerous it is?"

"You have no idea," Sarah said as she and her sister trudged out of the water, the wind blowing sand into their faces. It was like Somnambulus was having one last trick, although they knew that he was long gone. It was only the storm that made it so.

Their father came up with a towel. "Your mother is waiting in the car. They are evacuating the island. We need to get out of here quickly. Can you wait to change until we stop somewhere?"

"I think so," they said.

Sarah and Lily dried off a little and started to follow their father up the beach. They passed their sandcastle as they went. Nothing was left but the eroded outline of the keep, the canyon, and some of the outer walls. The tower, as they well knew, had fallen. Most of the outbuildings had returned to the ocean. As they watched, another wave crashed over it, blurring it even more. King Triton was making fast work of it now that he had his trident once again.

Sarah and Lily crossed to the sand dunes at the back of the beach, and then climbed the stairs to the wooden walkway that came from the hotel. They stopped to look back. On the horizon, they could see a little boat drifting into the darkness. Suddenly, out of the water they saw a head appear. It was Scallop! She waved at them one last time, blew them a kiss, and then dove back into the water. They stood for a moment, waving back.

"Who are you waving at?" their father asked them.

"Oh, just a friend we made," Sarah replied. She knew better than to try to convince grownups about the fairy world, for even if they experienced something supernatural, they soon forgot it.

The girls followed their father out into the parking lot and into the car. They had barely buckled up when water started falling out of the sky. The storm finally came in all its fury. They drove out of the hotel parking lot and down the road. As they went, they caught glimpses of the beach, with wind blowing sand into little clouds and waves crashing up high on the beach. Soon the waves would reach the buildings, sitting on their wooden piling to protect them from floods and hurricanes. The girls' family drove until they reached the highway, which was backed up with cars full of people trying to get off the island. They got in line with the others, slowly making their way out of the storm.

As they drove across the bridge, Sarah and Lily looked back. They could see in the storm clouds the features of the wizened face of King Triton, his beard billowing out in a large cloud. He was in charge of the sea again and was making quick work of his enemies – the Sand Wizard and the Sea Hag and their minions and servants. Sarah and Lily knew the battle had been won. Yet despite the threatening storm, with its strong winds blowing sand and debris across the road and its heavy rains, they knew they were safe. With his trident, Triton was ordering the seas again and would not allow them to come to harm. After another few minutes, they crossed the bridge and were off the island.

Sarah and Lily returned to their world, but as before, they continued to see the fairies in the most unusual places. Now that they had made friends with the merpeople, they started to see them, too, when they went to the beach, although their visits were few and far between.

Father knew that something had happened to them. He saw how brave they were in the face of danger. Later, when he saw them playing at their fairy games or pretending they were mermaids at the pool, he thought it was just that – a game – perhaps one they took very seriously and included a lot of details, but a game just the same. Yet ever afterwards, they feared no water, and he never had to worry about their safety. Their time with the merpeople and fairies had changed them for the better, just as his absence when he was gone to the war had made them stronger. For that, he was thankful.

# About the Author

J.D. Manders has been a technical writer and a historian for nearly twenty years. He is the author of *The Fairy Child*, which he wrote to connect with his children while deployed to Iraq in 2004. He finished *The Mermaid's Quest* for his children while deployed to Afghanistan in 2012. He has been a member of the U.S. Army National Guard since 1988. Since publishing *The Fairy Child*, he has been speaking widely to military families as an advocate of Family Readiness. He has been happily married for more than twenty years and has two wonderful daughters.